P9-DDS-114

Melinda Bannister is a brilliant scientist with an itch for dangerous lovers. Scratching that itch has put her into the blood-soaked hands of the mysterious mercenary assassin known only as Vancouver. He plans to auction her off to whichever terrorist group will pay top dollar for the right to pick her invaluable brain. The time bomb that is Melinda Bannister has begun to tick.

CONTE'S RUN

Vancouver claims to be the most deadly killer-for-hire in the world. But Dennison knows in his gut that Vancouver can be stopped—*must* be stopped. Someone has to take on the job, and when they call for volunteers, Dennison's Warriors are the only people with the guts to step forward. Dennison dispatches Matt Conte, veteran of the tropical jungle of Southeast Asia, and the asphalt jungle of New York's Mafia-controlled streets. Conte's assignment: hunt down the most ruthless killing machine on the globe, and stop him—dead.

DENNISON'S WAR

CONTE'S RUN

Adam Lassiter

BANTAM BOOKS
TORONTO · NEW YORK · LONDON · SYDNEY · AUCKLAND

DENNISON'S WAR: CONTE'S RUN
A Bantam Book / March 1985

ISBN 0-553-24588-0

Published simultaneously in the United States and Canada

Bantam Books are published by Bantam Books, Inc. Its trade-
mark, consisting of the words "Bantam Books" and the por-
trayal of a rooster, is Registered in U.S. Patent and Trademark
Office and in other countries. Marca Registrada. Bantam
Books, Inc., 666 Fifth Avenue, New York, New York 10103.

PRINTED IN THE UNITED STATES OF AMERICA

O   0 9 8 7 6 5 4 3 2 1

For 1983's Kids:

*Kelsey Rose Briggs, Benjamin John Tuholske,
and Elizabeth Woods Whiston*

The art of war is simple enough. Find out where your enemy is. Get at him as soon as you can. Strike at him as hard as you can and as often as you can, and keep moving on.

—Ulysses S. Grant

Monaco

The 3rd of August

Imagine a sociologist from an alien planet, landing on Earth to study its civilizations, and encountering, among a crowd, Burt Reynolds. The visiting scientist would not know that this man was famous, that he was universally considered a paradigm of manhood, virility, and physiological aesthetics, but if the scientist enjoyed reasonable powers of perception and observation, he would look at Burt Reynolds and compare him to the other Earthlings in the crowd, and think, *here is someone special; here is an extraordinary specimen.*

The woman was like that: beyond beautiful. She was lovely in a luminous, bedazzling way, like a perfectly cut diamond among an array of industrial-grade stones. People often mistook her for a film star; they would lean toward their companions and say, *sotto voce*, "I can't think of her name, but I know I saw her in that Coppola movie." Even here in Monte Carlo, where the alien sociologist might conclude from watching the tourists that handsomeness was

1

a prerequisite for a visa, the woman's magnificence was patently unique.

On this night she wore an evening gown of raw silk the color of buttermilk. It clung to her hips and the sweeping curve of her buttocks like an insecure lover's desperate embrace, then dwindled to two scarflike swatches that crisscrossed her full breasts before tying behind her neck, so the costume was backless and halfway to frontless as well. She could not have been wearing undergarments; the dress was so tight that a Band-Aid would have stuck out like a bas-relief.

The man with her was handsome, but in a conventional way: dark haired, broad shouldered, trim waisted, clean featured. He wore evening dress that had been perfectly done up earlier in this long night, but which was somewhat rumpled now. His tie was missing and his collar button undone, and one of the flaps of the jacket's pockets was tucked in and creased.

The moon was three-quarters full and sparkled off the white sand of the beach and the foam of the small waves lapping at it. They were walking just out of the water's reach. Above and behind them was the Place du Casino, the brightly lit white building shining like a multifaceted gem. Higher up on the foothills that pressed the principality up against the Mediterranean, across the French frontier, a few car headlights snaked back and forth over the switchback roads that climbed into the Maritime Alps. But here on the beach near the harbor, the late night was tranquil.

"I love this place," the woman said. "God, do I love this place."

She turned into the man's arms, and he crushed her close, so he could feel her full breasts swelling against his chest through the thin material of her dress. Immediately he felt himself hardening, and so did the woman, because her hand snaked down and began to rub at his crotch through his trousers. His mouth sucked hungrily at hers.

His hands moved lower on her bare back, but she pulled free, slowly and insistently, teasing the man. Holding his arm with one hand to steady herself, she reached down and pulled off her high heels, then ran the few steps to the water, bare feet splashing in the receding wave as she reared back and threw the shoes as far as she could. She waited for the faint splash, then laughed gaily. Perhaps she was a little drunk; they had been drinking champagne earlier.

She looked over her shoulder and called, "Come on."

"Hey," the man said weakly.

"Come on," the woman insisted, and she began to run on the hard sand, leaving a little wake as she splattered through the few inches of ocean at the beach's edge.

The man opened his mouth to call to her to stop and closed it again without speaking, knowing it would be futile. There was no stopping her when she got like this. He started after her in a dogtrot, already panting from the breathless kiss, or perhaps from his arousal. He passed another couple—the woman was black and had the regal features of an ancient Ethiopian queen—and felt vaguely foolish. After that, the beach was empty.

Ahead of him the woman disappeared behind a cliff-side boulder. He darted after her—and sprawled into the fine clean sand, tripped by her extended foot.

"Goddamn it," he snapped. He felt a little vulnerable in the face of her beauty and hated to appear ridiculous to her. He started to protest and to sit up, and accomplished neither as the woman flopped down on top of him, pressing all the length of her body against his, seeking out his mouth with her full lips. Her hair, blond and fine and pale as bone china, brushed his face like baby breath.

"I want you, Vin," the woman murmured. Her own

breath was warm, and touched at his skin like the fingers of a succubus. "I want you up inside me, deep enough to touch bottom."

They were mostly hidden from the beach by the jumble of cliff-break rocks, and to their back, the cutbank rose perhaps forty feet. The only sounds were regular and soothing: the soft rush of the tame surf, the vague murmur of traffic on the Avenue Princess Grace above them, the rise and fall of her inhalation and exhalation.

"We're right in the middle of . . ." the man began, without much conviction. She paid no attention to the words, and neither did his cock, coming almost immediately to hardness once more.

"There's no one to see," the woman crooned. "Please, Vin, I need you. I want you here."

She grabbed his hand and pressed it between her legs, and then she did something behind her neck and the two crisscrossed swatches of silk dropped away. Her breasts were tanned the same uniform brown as the rest of her, the nipples hard from the slight night chill and her passion.

"Or maybe someone *will* see, Vin," she went on, smooth and compelling as a hypnotist. Her hands moved over him, working at buckles and buttons and zippers. "They will watch everything we do. We'll pretend we don't know they are there, but we will, and we'll perform for them." She had his jacket off now, and was tugging his shirt over his shoulders. "Does that make you hot, Vin?"

He reached up to cup her breasts, one in each hand, and she let him knead gently at their fullness before pulling away once more. She stood for a moment and the rest of the silk gown fell away, and she stepped out of the little puddle of material and posed for him in the moonlight. Her body was exquisite.

"It makes me wet to think about it, Vin," she

whispered as she lay atop him again. "Feel how wet I am." She guided his hand into place.

The man was beyond nervousness or embarrassment or fear of discovery now, beyond anything but the undeniable need for the gorgeous woman and the succor and release of her lovemaking. He said nothing as she undid his pants and skinned them down over his ankles, and then he was as naked as she, feeling the soft sand against his back and butt, the breeze rustling through his chest hair and playing over his stiff erection.

She was on top of him again. Her skin felt almost electrically warm, and the moist hair between her thighs cradled his hardness as her lips nibbled his, her tongue explored the inside of his mouth.

After a while she began to move lower. She stopped to roll his nipples around with her tongue before tracing a warm, wet line down his sternum and stomach. Before she took his thickness into her mouth, she bunched her long blond hair in her left fist and pulled it out of her face. He liked to watch, and she liked him to.

The man began to whimper out his arousal, and his hips started to churn, at first spasmodically and then in rhythm to her bobbing movements, thrusting up to meet her mouth as she swallowed up most of his length.

Around him the woman was moaning out her own excitement now. She formed a ring with the thumb and forefinger of her free hand, and engirded him, moving it in tandem with her mouth and tongue and lips, more quickly now, then quicker still as the man's whimpers became urgent and then demanding, undeniable.

He grunted, a tortured animal sound, and the woman felt him swell in her mouth. Then the spasms began, and she tasted the salty thickness pulse down her throat.

At first, she sensed nothing wrong when he went limp,

but then it occurred to her that it had happened with unnatural quickness. His entire body was still, and she heard no postorgasmic gasp, no sound from him at all. She sensed it then, even shivered a little as she let his soft organ drop from her mouth and raised her head.

The side of the man's head was covered with a wash of red, matted in his hair and glistening darkly in the moonlight, and blood continued to pulse weakly from the hole in his temple. It dripped down in thin ropes to join the growing puddle in the sand. The man stared back at her through dead opaque eyes.

The woman scuttled away on all fours from this horror. One strand of her blond hair was glued to her wet lips, and she brushed it unconsciously aside before she opened her mouth to scream.

A hand clamped over it before any sound came out. The hand jerked her to her feet, her breasts swinging uncomfortably. She tried to twist free, and almost made it before being pulled back against a hard, clothed body. Something sharp jabbed into her bare buttocks. Within moments the drowsiness came on. The woman tried to fight it, but then fighting—against the cruel hand, against the urge to sleep—became too much trouble, and she drifted away from the living nightmare to somewhere else.

La Jolla, California

The 5th of August

From the veranda of the clubhouse, endless green fairways stretched off in every visible direction, the color under the cloudless spring sky almost brilliant enough to make Dennison squint. So when he and Miss Paradise entered the cocktail lounge inside, the contrast made the room seem dim to the point of being ill-lit, and it took the minute during which the maitre d' pretended not to notice them for Dennison's pupils to dilate enough for him to see into the room's deeper reaches.

The maitre d' was a tall, very slim man with an aquiline nose, narrow distant eyes, and a fastidious expression. He looked over Dennison and said, "Yes?" in the tone a housewife might use on opening the front door to discover an encyclopedia salesman about to go into his pitch.

"Mr. Bannister's table, please," Dennison said.

"Mr. Lawrence Bannister, the physicist?" the maitre d' said, as if it were a quiz question.

"No," Miss Paradise snapped. "Mr. Max Bannister, the bookmaker."

"He's expecting us," Dennison put in smoothly.

"More's the pity," the maitre d' murmured, meeting Miss Paradise's gaze. With nonmembers, he could get away with that sort of crap. But he turned, and they followed him as he wound among the tables to one in the far corner.

Dennison happened to know that the initiation fee for this particular club was $25,000, so he imagined its members were used to attractive women, but eyes still swiveled to follow Miss Paradise across the room. She loved to dress up in costumes, and on this day she wore jodhpurs, a khaki blouse, a neckerchief, and a safari hat. "Maureen O'Sullivan," Dennison had guessed in the helicopter on the way over. "In *Tarzan, the Ape Man,* before she goes native with Weissmuller."

"Wrong again, boss." She loved to stymie him in his game. "Mary Astor in *Red Dust,* vamping Clark Gable."

Now, in the golf club's cocktail lounge, she glided across the room like a tall ship. Her height was exactly six feet, and she had long hair the color of electrum and the lanky flowing figure of a high-fashion model. Nominally she was Dennison's secretary, but sometimes it was she who made the rules, and one of them which she enforced religiously was that he went nowhere without her.

Dennison was dressed as if he might have just changed in the locker room after a brisk eighteen holes, in casual slacks, an open-necked polo shirt, and slip-on deck shoes. The maitre d' stepped aside and said, "Mr. Lawrence Bannister," like a courtier announcing the arrival of a plenipotentiary.

Bannister rose and offered his hand, first to Dennison and then to Miss Paradise. Dennison knew the man was in his early thirties, but by appearance he might have been five years younger, or ten years older. He had tightly curled dark hair that was beginning to recede, and an ascetic, almost gaunt face with worry creases at the corners of his eyes. For all that, he was not an unattractive man. He was about Miss Paradise's height, and he had the casually thrown-back shoulders and graceful bearing of a person for whom athletics of some kind had been a part of routine since childhood. Dennison imagined that on the tennis or racquetball court he would be a fierce competitor.

"Thank you for coming," Bannister said. "Please, sit." A waiter materialized out of the dimness. "What would you like?"

Dennison ordered a Martel Five Star brandy highball with soda, and Miss Paradise a glass of chilled Chablis. Bannister tapped a fingernail against the glass in front of him, empty except for a few melting ice cubes, and the waiter murmured, "Thank you, Mr. Bannister," and drifted back into the shadows.

Bannister clasped his hands together on the table in front of him and leaned forward. "Have you found anything out?"

"Yeah," Miss Paradise said. "We found out you lied to us."

"That's not true."

"I'm afraid it is." Dennison's tone was rueful, as if the thought that anyone would do such a thing pained him deeply. "You deliberately left out important information. You misled me, which is the same as a lie in my business."

"I'm willing to pay whatever you wish, Mr. Dennison. I explained that to you."

"And I explained to you that I expected straight answers."

Bannister started to reply, but then the waiter returned with the drinks. Bannister carelessly initialed a bar tab, then gulped down half his highball in one swallow. "Please," he said, his voice a little raw from the whiskey or emotion, "have you found my wife?"

"No," Miss Paradise said coldly. "And until you come clean with us, there isn't much chance we will."

Although silent air-conditioning made the air of the cocktail lounge crisp as iceberg lettuce, there was a visible sheen of moisture on Bannister's clean-shaven upper lip. Dennison regarded the man over the rim of his own glass. He met him almost exactly forty-eight hours earlier when Bannister had arrived at Dennison's isolated mountainside compound by helicopter, the only way in. He needed help on a matter of great delicacy, Bannister told Dennison in his office. Dennison had been recommended by a man serving in a middle-management position at the Department of State; Bannister met him ten years earlier, when both were in Military Intelligence. Dennison knew the man at State only casually, but it was introduction enough for him to at least hear Bannister out.

He was a physicist and an electronics engineer who specialized in microcircuitry, Bannister told Dennison. But that had nothing to do with the matter at hand, he added quickly.

"It's my wife, Melinda," Bannister had said.

"Lots of times it is," Miss Paradise murmured.

Bannister shot her a glance. "This isn't easy for me." He fished a straight-stemmed pipe from his inside jacket pocket, but made no move to fill its bowl. "For several months Melinda has been carrying on an affair with a man named Andrew V. Dana. He operates some sort of import/ export business out of a storefront office in Seattle's Union Square district; I don't know much more about him than that."

Miss Paradise had a stenographer's pad out, but Dennison knew that was for show. If necessary, she was capable of repeating verbatim a half-hour conversation, two days after it took place.

"A little more than a week ago," Bannister went on, "my wife disappeared. I subsequently found out that Dana's office had been closed on the same day."

"You hired a private investigator?"

"That's correct. He was helpful to a point, but now I feel I need more . . . specialized skills than he was able to offer."

"What do you want me to do, Mr. Bannister?" Dennison asked. He sat slightly slumped in his chair, his hands folded on his stomach.

"Find my wife and bring her back to me."

"What if she doesn't want to come back?" Miss Paradise asked.

"I—I—I feel confident she will," Bannister stammered.

It was a poor answer, and all three of them knew it, but Dennison had not chosen to press the point. Instead he nodded and smiled faintly, and said, "My fee will be three hundred thousand dollars, Mr. Bannister. My terms are payment in advance and no refunds under any circumstances. Once the assignment begins it will be carried through to whatever I consider a satisfactory conclusion—even if you should change your mind. There are certain risks involved in my business. We assume sole responsibility for our actions, without bringing you into the picture in any way. In return we get a free hand."

Bannister paled. Then he replaced the cold pipe in his pocket, brought out a leather-covered folder, and said steadily, "I assume my personal check is acceptable?"

"Right off we knew your story had a funny smell," Miss Paradise was saying now, in the corner of the dimly lit lounge. She dug a soft pack of Marlboros from her bag and used a Bic disposable lighter on one. "We didn't like the part about your buddy from the old MI days—although you were smart enough to give a name that we'd recognize. Also, you knew too much about this Dana character not to know more—unless the investigator you hired was a complete dolt, he would have asked around Dana's office building, found out what kind of hours he kept, how much he traveled, what sort of people came and went. That's the first thing they teach you in detective school."

"Then there was the money," Dennison picked up. "*Time* magazine says that electronics professionals draw good salaries these days, but three hundred thousand dollars is a lot for most people."

"Especially since if the job was as simple as you said," Miss Paradise added, "a competent investigator could have found your wife in two weeks tops, at no more than five hundred a day plus expenses." From her bag she took a spiral-bound notebook, which she handed to the boss. Dennison flipped it open and scanned the first page.

The waiter glided up to the table, and Miss Paradise ordered another glass of wine. Dennison smiled up at the man and shook his head. Bannister ordered a double of whatever he was drinking.

"After the way you blew smoke at us," Dennison said, "we decided that if we wanted the truth, we'd have to find it out ourselves."

The waiter picked up the ashtray in front of Miss Paradise, spotless except for a one-quarter-inch cylinder of ash, and replaced it with a clean one, then sailed away.

"Why?" Bannister asked. "If you knew I lied to you—or at least held back—why didn't you just refuse my check?"

Across the room at the bar a youngish man slid from

his stool to demonstrate for a buddy his driver swing, for which he held his imaginary club cross-handed. He brought the imaginary head back in a shoulder-wrenching back-swing, then drew it smoothly through the plane of the imaginary ball, like Johnny Carson at the end of his monologue. He bowed extravagantly, then held out a palms-up hand to his friend, as if saying, "You try."

Dennison looked back to the nervous Bannister, who was staring at the open notebook as if it were his rap sheet. "Curiosity," Dennison answered. "Call it a hunch. That and the fact that you were obviously a badly frightened man."

Dennison glanced again at the notebook. "Calling yourself an electronics engineer is like calling Ronald Reagan a retired actor. You are the director and principal stockholder in a privately held corporation, Bannister Systems Technology of Bellevue, across Lake Washington from Seattle. BST was founded forty-one years ago by your father, who began his professional career as a research assistant to Eckert and Mauchly on the UNIVAC I project, during which time your father made some valuable government contacts. An expert in R&D involving computers and robotics, your father broke away to form BST, whose only client for the last ten years has been the U.S. government. Since your father's death from a heart attack in the mid-seventies, you have run the company and done well enough to maintain a summer home here as well as your permanent residence in Bellevue. You're a rich man, Bannister."

Dennison flipped to the next page. "Andrew Vincent Dana, age thirty-four, is a U.S. citizen by birth and a onetime engineering major at California Polytechnic State University. After graduating with two degrees he worked for several high-tech companies on the West Coast, most recently as a senior programmer. He lost his last job after he was accused of stealing and selling trade secrets. The accusation was supported by hard evidence, but Dana wasn't prosecuted because if he was brought into court, his testimony would reveal those same secrets. The company had to settle for getting rid of him and then spreading the word within the professional community, so Dana would never work in the field again."

A pretty redheaded woman in Bermuda shorts and anklets as purely white as a deacon's conscience had joined the driving seminar at the bar. The first young man was standing behind her with his hands reached around to guide her wrists. The woman was giggling; she knew what was going on and liked it a lot.

"Dana had a marketable skill," Miss Paradise said, sounding to Dennison a little impatient, "but no place where he could use it to make a living. So he hit on the idea of setting up as a free lance and continuing to do what he had as an employee. Supposedly he was a consultant; in fact he was an industrial spy, stealing and selling computerized data."

"Dana began by peddling his information to competing firms in this country," Dennison said, turning another page. "Pretty quickly he realized he could make more money with overseas clients—selling them top secret national defense technology."

"The punk was a traitor." Miss Paradise ground out her cigarette in the middle of the immaculate ashtray, where the golf club's coat of arms was embossed.

"How did you discover all this so quickly?" Bannister asked.

"We've got sources." Dennison smiled. "That's one of the reasons you're paying us a lot of money. It turns out that the FBI and the CIA have had Dana under surveillance for some time—since right after he was fired from his last job, in fact. Most of what I just told you was developed through their intelligence information. But none of this is news to you, is it, Bannister?"

Bannister stalled by taking a drink. "As chief executive officer of BST, I have a top security clearance. It's required for the type of R&D we do for Defense. I used my own contacts to learn most of what you just told me, yes."

"That's also how you got Dennison's name," Miss Paradise said. "That business about your old army buddy was a bucket of eyewash, right?"

"Yes," Bannister said to his drink.

"The FBI and the CIA knew that Dana's foreign clients included unfriendly nations. In plain language, Dana was selling military secrets to the enemy: Third World dictatorships, Soviet client states, even independent terrorist organizations. That's the man your wife decided to run off with."

"That's bad enough," Dennison pointed out, "but it gets worse. Tell us about her, Bannister."

"You seem to know all about it already, Dennison."

"I'd like to hear your version," Dennison said in the same even, calm voice.

Lawrence Bannister picked up his glass and wiped a finger absently across the wet ring it left on the hardwood tabletop. Across the room the pretty redheaded woman was leaving with the guy who hit golf balls cross-handed. She looked even more pleased, and *why not*? Dennison thought; there were worse ways to spend a spring Tuesday. Some people even had to work. . . .

"In addition to being my wife," Bannister said tonelessly, "Melinda is my full business partner. She has a doctorate from MIT, and she collaborates on all our projects."

"She has the same clearance as you?"

"Certainly. Melinda is a brilliant scientist—and she is absolutely loyal to this country." Bannister gave Dennison a hard look. "Any suggestion to the contrary is absurd, not to mention libelous."

"That may be so," Miss Paradise said, "but she's run off with a traitor. She could be the direct descendant of Paul Revere and it still wouldn't look good for her."

"She must have been kidnapped," Bannister said, as if he had just thought of the notion and liked it quite a bit.

"That could be," Dennison said. He dropped his voice to a confidential, man-to-man level. "Dana wasn't the first guy, was he?"

"Shit," Bannister said surprisingly. He raised his glass and said, "Fernando," not much louder than they had been speaking. But the waiter was at the table instantly, like a genie from a bottle. Bannister ordered another double.

"My wife is a profoundly intelligent woman," he said. "She is capable of some of the most incredibly imaginative leaps of theoretical research I have ever witnessed, and yet her talent seems effortless. She could have been a success in anything she chose to take up.

"Unfortunately," Bannister went on, "she is also curious, headstrong, often restless—perhaps a result of her genius. Her attention span is not long."

Bannister grabbed his drink from the waiter's tray before he could place it in front of him. He downed half of it, and when he went on his voice had finally begun to slur a little.

"Which is a sophisticated way of saying, yeah, Melinda has something of an itch for anything in pants." Bannister laughed unpleasantly. "She's had a few affairs— since we met, before we were married, afterwards, ever since. The interesting part—from a scientist's view, you understand—is that she is primarily attracted to men quite different from herself."

"What kind of men?" Dennison asked.

"Dangerous men. Not too dangerous, but dangerous enough to give her a thrill. Motorcycle bums, urban cowboys, cocaine dealers—that sort of halfway outlaw. She is a hedonist, and that doesn't jibe with a career in the hard sciences. So she has invented for herself a parallel life, as carefree and wild as her science is disciplined."

Dennison's own glass was still half full. He took a shallow sip of the now-watery brandy. "What was she working on when she disappeared?"

"That's top secret," Bannister said with half-drunk shrewdness.

"Listen, Bannister," Dennison said, coldly and with no hint of his smile. "You wasted my time once. Don't even try it a second time."

"A television," Bannister muttered sullenly.

"I beg your pardon?"

"She was working on a television."

"It must be some television for BST to be involved," Miss Paradise said. "What does it do, automatically tune out any comedy featuring a cute kid?"

"Cathode-ray-tube technology has had important defense applications since its birth," Bannister said primly, like a college lecturer. "Most recently it has been used in intelligent air-to-ground missiles. A camera in the nose sends back signals to a monitor in the cockpit, which the pilot uses to guide the missile to target. The problems are—or were—lack of resolution, which is a fancy way of saying it was a lousy picture, and with hidden targets—if the missile can't see them, then neither can the pilot and he is out of luck.

"BST is working on a new high-resolution system that

will solve most of the problem and open entirely new fields of application. Let me give you one rather flashy example: picture a fleet of pilotless planes—warplanes, cargo ships, whatever—all 'flown' by one man on the ground sitting in front of a bank of monitors showing everything over a full sphere of vision, along with readings from the plane's monitoring system."

"Pretty handy," Miss Paradise said.

Bannister looked from her to Dennison. "Please, I've told you everything you wished to know. Now you must tell me what you've found out about Melinda."

Dennison put his palms flat on the table. "Do you love your wife, Mr. Bannister?"

"Of course I do."

"But the primary reason you need her back," Dennison pressed, "is that if the story we've just told each other gets out, you're finished, professionally, financially, and every other way."

"That is abs—"

"The FBI and the CIA know that Dana has disappeared. So far they don't know your wife went with him; they don't even know she's gone. But if they learn she's been playing house with a turncoat punk like Andrew Vincent Dana, they'll be very unhappy, and very nervous—and the first thing they'll do is revoke the security clearance of her, you, and BST. You'll be out of business, and when the word gets out in the industry, you won't be able to get a job repairing digital watches. That's why you had to come to me instead of the authorities."

For a long time Bannister stared back at him, and Dennison wondered if the man was finally drunk beyond the point of rationally continuing this conversation. But when he spoke it was in a voice that was calm and reasoned, and touched with a note of genuine sincerity.

"What you say is true. It is also true that I love Melinda utterly and absolutely. I think she loves me as well. I do know she respects me, and perhaps that's closer to love than most men get with a woman who looks like Melinda."

He chugged back the last of his drink. "Find her, Dennison. Find her and bring her back, and give me that one last chance."

Dennison pursed his lips and saw out of the corner of his eye that Miss Paradise was watching him closely. Lawrence Bannister might be a brilliant scientist and a genius, but he was dumb as a schoolboy about the facts of real life. He was the kind who would always be respected by his colleagues and kicked in the face by his women.

But none of that was Dennison's concern. He had decided to go on with the job before arriving at this place. There was the money, of course; there was always the money. But there was a more immediate consideration.

The time bomb that was Melinda Bannister had begun to tick.

From the back of the notebook Dennison removed a newspaper clipping, unfolded it, and smoothed it on the tabletop, then passed it to Bannister. It had been cut from an inside page of the *International Herald Tribune,* and filled no more than six column inches.

AMERICAN TOURIST
FOUND ON BEACH

(Monaco)—The nude body of an American tourist who had been shot once in the head was found on the beach three hundred yards from the Place du Casino early yesterday morning when a

jogger's dog apparently stopped to investigate an
unfamiliar scent.

The man was traveling under the name of
Vincent Dana Andrews, although unofficial police
sources say this was an alias. The sources would
not speculate on the victim's real name, nor the
reason for the alias.

Andrews was shot with a .22 caliber weapon
apparently fitted with a silencer, since police
received no reports of gunfire. He is believed to
have died instantly.

Andrews and a woman identified as his wife
were registered at the Lido, according to a
management spokesman, although the woman has
subsequently disappeared. Her personal belong-
ings, as well as those of Andrews, were left
behind and were undisturbed.

Police are seeking Mrs. Andrews for questioning. She is described as a striking blond
woman, height about . . .

Bannister slowly looked up from the article. "Have—
have they found her?"

Dennison shook his head no.

"But this means . . ." Bannister stopped himself.
"You will look for her, Mr. Dennison, won't you?"

"She may be dead," Dennison said, his tone muted.

Bannister drew himself more erect. "But you don't
believe she is."

Bannister was right; Dennison believed that Melinda
alive was worth a lot of money to a lot of people. But all he
said was, "I have no idea."

"One way or the other," Bannister said. "One way or the other I want to know."

Bannister's eyes were wet, his voice barely under control, and suddenly Dennison wanted very much not to be present if the man broke down. He stood abruptly, Miss Paradise fluidly following suit. Bannister had been booted around by his wife all their life together, but Dennison felt only pity for the man—and that was a long way from sympathy.

"Good-bye, Bannister," he said. "Thanks for the drink."

"She does love me, Dennison," Bannister choked. "That is the God's truth."

But there was no good response to that, and Dennison took Miss Paradise's arm and guided her past the supercilious maitre d' and back out into the forgotten sunshine.

BOOK ONE

Conte's Way

Chapter One

The girl behind the counter in the gift shop off the lobby of El San Juan resort could not have been older than fifteen. She had coffee-colored skin and a soft round body still layered with a bit of baby fat, but she was quite pretty, and would be beautiful when she grew willowy and the braces came off her teeth. She laughed shyly at nothing at all when Matthew Conte came up to the counter, and though she tried to laugh with her mouth shut Conte caught the flash of the metal.

"Camels, *por favor*," Conte said.

The girl giggled again and fetched the cigarettes from a rack behind her. The rack had a Salem logo atop it, and a picture of a supremely Aryan blond woman, in wet hair and a bikini, head thrown back as she sucked on her mentholated smoke.

Conte put two dollar bills on the counter and gestured, so the girl would know the change was for her. "*Gracias,*" Conte said, which used up his Spanish vocabulary.

The girl laughed once more, covering her mouth with the back of her hand.

"Someday you'll have the straightest teeth on this island," Conte told her. The girl said, "*Gracias, señor.*" Even if she had no idea what he said, she recognized the compliment. He liked that. He felt good these days, healthy and at ease, and for him there were not too many times like that.

Matt Conte was an assassin. It was not a profession that lent itself to relaxation.

He broke the seal of the pack of cigarettes, tamped one out against the side of his hand, and lit it with a gold Zippo. Across the lobby, the hotel's casino was starting to fill, although it was summer and should have been the off-season for Puerto Rico. East Coast folk, tired of the painted-lady tawdriness of Atlantic City and down for a long weekend of gambling, Conte figured.

Conte didn't blame them. San Juan was one of his favorite casino towns. The gaming rooms were quiet and elegant and businesslike; unlike Vegas, there were no six-foot-tall waitresses wearing one-foot-tall hairdos and scanty togas, or trapeze artists performing over the crap tables, and only rarely did you see a woman with blue hair and heart-shaped sunglasses clutching a Dixie cup of nickels and staring like a charmed cobra at the whirling windows of a slot machine. Hell, once in a while a dealer even smiled at a mark; in Nevada that was a firing offense.

At the second crap table a woman had the dice. She was in her mid-forties and very handsome, with bare broad shoulders above an evening dress, and an open face with a mouth that came within a few millimeters of being horsey, but managed to miss; she looked sleek and healthy and corn fed. Conte played the pass line, betting with the woman for luck, and won when she came out with a seven. He was not here for craps, but it was an old and deeply ingrained habit to get the feel of any newly entered place. Conte had learned long ago to always know what was at his back.

He won two more small bets before the woman

crapped out, and he declined the dice. He had picked up his twenty dollars in winnings and was turning from the table when she put a light hand on his arm. "You owe me a drink." A broad midwestern accent flavored the woman's voice, a rich contralto. "You won all that money on my dice."

Conte held up the two green ten-dollar chips and rubbed them together. "Can't." He smiled. "I've got the itch. I'm holding money that's dying to be gambled."

"Compulsive, huh?" The woman gave back the smile. "That's me, too. Maybe we should team up."

"I always work alone."

"Some things take two."

Up close she was pretty, in a mature-lady kind of way. Her skin was clear and nut brown, not a two-week tourist tan but a color that told of regular acquaintance with high bright sun. She was wearing some kind of scent, but it smelled fresh, not flowery.

"Nebraska?" Conte asked.

"Kansas." Her hand was still on his arm. "Mabel Jones—don't make any funny remarks," she added quickly. "I'm planning on changing it when I get around to it."

"To what?"

"Mabel Smith."

Conte laughed. "Listen . . ."

Mabel Jones cut him off. "I'm a widow," she said solemnly. "The hubby had a heart attack. He was milking, and he keeled over, right off the stool. I found him with his face in the bucket. He left me the farm."

"Sorry," Conte murmured.

"Don't be. It happened in 1972. How about that drink?"

Conte was having a good time, but he shook his head. "Maybe later."

"I'll be around." She brushed very close to him, the nipple of one ample breast grazing his shoulder. Conte watched her cruise out of the casino.

When he turned around, he came face-to-face with the past.

The shift had changed at the crap table where Mabel Jones had been rolling, and Matt Conte knew the new croupier. He was called Weepy Moyers—if he'd once had a given first name, no one could remember it—and the last time Conte had seen him was about four months earlier, in Reno in a joint called the Golden Lady. Weepy had been a pit boss then, so it looked like he had come down a peg in the gambling world.

Weepy caught Conte's eye and gave him the office: be with you a little later, the gesture said. That was fine with Matt Conte. All that interested him was a little recreational gambling, and anyway, Weepy Moyers was pretty far from his idea of a bosom buddy.

It was about ten o'clock now, and the casino was filling to capacity. The middle seat was open at one of the $100-limit blackjack tables, and Conte took it. He fished a sheaf of bills from his jacket pocket, removed a clip, and laid them in a pile in front of him: ten $100 bills. The dealer fanned them like a poker hand, shuffled them together, flipped chips into little piles from the tray in front of him, slid the piles to Conte's place. The dealer was a slim, handsome Latino with tightly curled hair and slender fingers, which he used with the effortless stylized grace of a Japanese chef. The cards seemed to leap from the dealing shoe into them, before flying through the air to land faceup precisely in front of each player. Conte put a red twenty-dollar chip in the square in front of him and drew a ten-deuce to the dealer's king up, but when Conte tapped a fingernail on the green baize he drew an eight. The dealer flipped a seven and paid Conte's twenty, a matching red chip scaling through the air to land beside the first, the dealer's accuracy as arcane as telekinesis.

In the seventh seat—"third base," the gamblers called it—a pretty blond woman split aces and drew two face cards for blackjacks. "*Buena, señorita,*" the dealer said without looking at her. The woman murmured, "*Gracias,*" but she was watching Conte. Conte smiled back—and then gave his attention to the matter at hand.

Blackjack was Conte's favorite casino game because it was the only one where the player sometimes had an edge over the house. Conte was a card counter; he used a simple point system to keep track of the way the composition of the four decks shuffled together in the dealing shoe changed. When a lot of ten-cards and aces were left, the odds shifted to favor the player, and Conte upped his bets.

Yet two hours—and four club sodas and a half-pack of Camels—after he sat down, he was only about even on the night. The deck had turned hot only three times in that span, and even then the individual cards had not come Conte's way. Sometimes that happened; everything was based on the long run. Still, he was getting a little impatient by the time Weepy Moyers appeared at his shoulder.

"How they running, Mattie? Hey, I got a twenty-minute break," he went on, without waiting for an answer. "You wanna cup of coffee?"

"Why not?" Conte gathered up his little pile of chips and dropped them in his jacket pocket. Mabel Jones was back at the second dice table, and Conte stopped and dropped a green chip on the pass line. The big corn-fed woman reared back and threw a six, then made it the hard way on the next roll. "That's two drinks you owe me, friend," she said across the table to Conte.

"I'll be back." Conte picked up the two chips and followed Weepy Moyers into the lobby.

Weepy seemed a little too glad to see him, which made Conte curious enough to overcome his distaste of the little man, at least until he found out what was on his mind. In Reno, Conte had to lean on the guy to get information, but now Weepy was bubbling over with talk—which meant he either needed a favor or was hedging against some time in the future when he would need one.

"Hey, Mattie, you are looking good." They were in a booth toward the back of the hotel coffee shop, which was mostly empty this early.

"What are you doing here, Weepy?" Conte said evenly.

The soft spaniel eyes from which Weepy took his nickname turned virtually lachrymose. "Hey, you know. A change is good for a guy."

"Good for the health?"

Weepy shrugged and looked away. "You kind of screwed me over in Reno, Mattie. You owe me one."

"Is that how you figure it?" Conte said coldly. He got out a cigarette and rolled it between thumb and forefinger.

"Don't get me wrong." Moyers took out a disposable lighter and lit Conte's cigarette for him. "I ain't asking for anything. I got some things you might want to know, is all. You know what happened back in Nevada."

In Nevada, Conte had been looking for a man named Frank Bressio, for a number of reasons. One of them was that Bressio had posted a price of $100,000 for Conte's head—with or without his body attached. Bressio had sicced a hired gun named Rudy Marcoux on Conte, but Rudy Marcoux had turned up cold as a TV dinner in a stable at the Reno Fairgrounds, after a long night of interrogation at Conte's hands. Marcoux had not died prettily.

But before he went, Marcoux had told Conte enough to lead him to Bressio, and now the onetime renegade crime boss was on ice as well. That was what had happened in Nevada; it was in the springtime.

"Of all the guys in town," Weepy said over his coffee, "you hadda buttonhole me."

"You didn't tell me anything," Conte pointed out.

"That don't make any difference to those boys. You know what they say: 'If it walks like a stoolie and smells like a stoolie and talks like a stoolie—'"

"—it is a duck," Conte finished.

"Huh?" Weepy knit brows over his moist eyes.

"Forget it."

"Sure." But Weepy stared at Conte suspiciously. "Anyway, I was getting the idea that Reno was hazardous to my health. No one took shots at me or nothing—they just gimme the idea that maybe it was time to move on. What the hell." Weepy shrugged philosophically. "I ain't no guy to be looking back."

"You've got one eye looking over your shoulder in your sleep," Conte said rudely.

"Hey, no hard feelings, Mattie," Weepy said quickly. "I'm no guy to hold a grudge."

Conte laughed.

"All right," Weepy said with some heat. "There's what I get for trying to do a pal a favor." He pushed his coffee away and stood up.

Conte looked up at him. For maybe ten seconds Weepy did not move. Then he sat down again.

"I'm listening," Conte said.

"You got a lot of brass, Mattie," Weepy said defiantly.

"Everyone knows that. 'That Conte, he's got a lot of brass.' That's what they say."

"Right. I've got a lot of brass. Speak your piece, Weepy."

"Maybe what you got is too much brass for your own good." He watched Conte blow out smoke in a thin stream that broke up to spiral toward the ceiling fan. "Just because Bressio is out of the picture don't mean the heat is off you."

"What's that supposed to mean?"

"It means the Old Men . . ." But then Weepy only shrugged again. "You know how the Old Men are."

The Old Men were the members of the Mafia's ruling council. Based in New York, they were the ultimate arbiters of anything that involved organized crime. The primary purpose of the council was to assure that business ran smoothly: that no one operated outside his territory, or became involved in the kind of violent or flamboyant crimes that brought attention to the Mob. The Old Men were like the board of directors of any large conglomerate—except that the businesses of this conglomerate ranged from loan-sharking to protection, gambling, drugs, prostitution, and occasionally murder.

Matthew Conte had worked for the Old Men— particularly for the crime-family boss Philip Agricola—for nearly ten years. Now Agricola was dead, assassinated by one of Frank Bressio's men before Conte brought Bressio to his knees, and Matt Conte was no longer associated with the Mob.

"You ever know anyone who quit clean?" Weepy Moyers said, as if he had heard Conte's thoughts. "Think about it, Mattie."

"Keep talking."

"The word on the street is, the Old Men okayed Mattie Conte's retirement, so don't turn tough with Mattie unless you want the Old Men breathing on you real hard. That's the word."

"Except you hear different," Conte guessed.

"What I hear," Weepy said, "is the Old Men never like the idea of one of their ex-boys running around loose. Even someone who has got a rep for being trustworthy and keeping his trap shut, like you, Mattie. Ex-boys always know too much, they're too smart. The Old Men hate smart guys."

That was another thing Conte knew full well. His father had been a smart guy—but not as smart as he thought. In his mind Conte carried a picture of his father as he had seen him last, almost fifteen years ago: lying on the dirty plank floor in the storeroom of his lower Manhattan corner store, blood puddled thick as varnish all around his corpse.

"I'm not saying there's paper out, Mattie," Weepy Moyers was going on. "The Old Men haven't issued a contract on you, near as I can tell. But I hear that maybe their attitude has changed a little; so they wouldn't be too broke up if some kind of accident happened to you."

Conte felt suddenly weary. It came with the territory— this business of big men with big guns always apt to pop up at your back. Conte knew and accepted that fact of life. But to be reminded of it from a little sad-eyed puppy like Weepy Moyers was something he could do without.

"Hey, Mattie," Weepy said. "You don't have to worry about me. I'm like a clam."

"That's a relief," Conte said. "Take a walk, Weepy."

"Hey, there's no call to be that way. I'm trying to do you a favor."

"Fade, Weepy. Dust on out of here."

Weepy Moyers pushed back his chair too hard and

stood up, scowling furiously. He started past the table, then changed his mind. He bent, his voice low.

"You got a fuck of a chip on your shoulder, Mattie."

Conte let go of his coffee cup and backhanded the little croupier across the mouth. Only his arm moved, but it was a hard blow, hard enough so that Weepy stumbled back into a chair. The chair went over, and Weepy went down on one knee.

The waitress looked up from where she was adding up a bill at the counter, and started toward them. Weepy got up quickly, straightened the chair. His lower lip was split, and there was a little blood on his chin. He dug out a handkerchief, dabbed at it, all the time staring at Conte. But he didn't say anything more, only turned on his heel and went out of there.

Losing his temper like that had been a stupid, bullying thing to do—and the hell with it, Conte thought. He was on vacation. He finished his coffee and dropped a five-dollar chip on the table. In the men's room he splashed a double handful of cold water in his face, patted it dry with the spotless white towel the attendant handed him, recombed his hair, and dropped a tip in the ashtray by the basin.

It was almost two in the morning by now, and the casino crowd was beginning to thin out. Weepy Moyers was careful to avoid his eyes when Conte passed, but Mabel Jones hollered out a cheerful, "Howdy, Bright Eyes. You ready for that drink." Conte stopped long enough to say, "Getting there," and watch her roll three naturals in a row. There was a jumbled pile of chips in front of her; Conte put the amount at around three grand.

The same handsome, deft dealer was presiding at the $100 blackjack table. There were only two players, and one of them left as Conte took the middle seat. Conte preferred a table with empty seats on either side, because in Puerto Rico the house let you play as many hands as were open. So when the deck went hot, Conte could get more action at an open table.

For a while it looked like his luck had not changed; the cards were lukewarm as boarding house soup. Conte bided his time with five-dollar minimum bets, and watched the dealer's fine hands manipulate the pasteboards.

Then, about a half hour after he sat down, the deck went very strong. Conte had been counting closely, and he knew that with half the quadruple deck gone, the remaining cards were nearly all aces and tens.

He sifted through the pile of chips before him, separated three black ones, and bet the limit of $100 on each of three hands. The other player, a middle-aged balding man in glasses who looked like a history professor, must have been a counter as well; he covered two squares with a black chip each.

The dealer's fine hands began to dispense cards—and behind Conte a familiar voice said brightly, "How they running for you, Hot Shot?"

Conte turned on his stool and looked up into the cocky grin of Miss Paradise.

The grin did not hold his attention long. Miss Paradise's long form was dressed—or half-dressed—in a two-piece outfit. The top was a simple bandeau that left a breathtaking expanse of bare shoulder above and ironing-board-flat stomach below; the bottom was an ankle-length swath of some kind of shimmery material that clung to her body like Ishmael clung to Queequeg's coffin.

Beside her stood Dennison, in a fawn-colored tropical-weight suit, smiling pleasantly. "Hello, Matt," he said.

"What are you doing here?" Conte asked the tall woman.

"Bringing you luck. You're glad to see us, right?"

Behind Conte the slim Latino announced, "*Viente y uno, señor.*" He flipped an ace atop his queen, and Conte's three $100 chips disappeared into the dealer's tray. All three of Conte's hands were twenties; the other man had a fourth twenty and a blackjack of his own, for a standoff. He glanced at Conte and shrugged, almost apologetically.

Despite all the ten-cards in the hand, by Conte's count the deck was still slewed in his favor. He covered the same three squares, one black chip each. The other man dropped his bet to $25 and played a single hand.

"That's the spirit," Miss Paradise said in Conte's ear. "Don't let 'em buffalo you."

The handsome dealer's hands were poised over the shoe, motionless. He was staring at Miss Paradise with unabashed awe, like a man who has just seen the face of Jesus appear among clouds.

"Batter up," Conte murmured.

The dealer blinked. "*Perdoneme, señor.*" A flurry of cards began to hit the felt. Conte's first two hands were twenties; the third was an ace and an eight for nineteen. The dealer showed a king.

The dealer flipped his hole card: a six. Impassive, smooth as veneer, he drew from the shoe—and flipped a five.

"*Viente y uno, señor.*"

"Can you take a break, Matt?" Dennison said courteously.

Conte pushed away from the table. "I'd better," he muttered. He gathered his chips in one hand, separated out a purple twenty-five and tossed it to the dealer, dumped the rest in his pocket.

The dealer didn't even glance at it. He was staring at Miss Paradise again. "*Señorita,*" he said softly.

"Yes?"

The dealer smiled, flashing brilliantly white teeth. "*Buenas noches,*" he said softly.

Miss Paradise smiled back. The professorial player was tapping his fingernails on the felt.

Dennison took Miss Paradise's elbow. "Come along, my dear."

The cocktail lounge had one missing wall that opened on the patio around the pool, overlooking the beach. They took an umbrellaed table at the end; at this hour of the early morning the temperature was in the low seventies, and there was a soft offshore breeze. Dennison ordered a Martel Five Star brandy and soda, and Miss Paradise a piña colada, which arrived with a ring of pineapple over the lip of the glass and a paper parasol sticking out of it. Conte had his eighth club soda of the evening.

"Still off the sauce?" Miss Paradise asked.

"I was never on it."

"How are you, Matt?" Dennison asked.

"I'm fine." Conte looked into his glass and said, "How's Chris?"

Miss Paradise laughed. "I didn't know you cared." Conte didn't bother to respond. He knew she was pleased that he and Chris Amado were getting along. There had been a time . . .

Dennison leaned forward. "Matt," he said in a low, even voice. "I need you."

"I thought you might," Conte said.

He listened without interrupting while Dennison told him about Lawrence Bannister and his wayward wife, Melinda. Halfway through the story he reached across the table and plucked the rice-paper parasol from Miss Paradise's glass, and he was twirling it between thumb and forefinger when Dennison finished his story.

"Questions?" Dennison said.

"Two. What are the chances Melinda Bannister is alive—and how great a threat does she pose if she is?"

"The second answer first: a lot of people—not the good guys, either—would pay a lot of money for what she can tell them, and the security of our national defense systems would be in real trouble. It isn't that she knows so much—in fact she only worked on four projects in the ten years she's been with Bannister and BST. But what information she could provide would supply a key to a lot more."

"When you're doing a jigsaw," Miss Paradise said, "first you separate out all the straight-edge pieces and fit them together to make the frame. From there you're halfway home. Think of Melinda Bannister's knowledge as the straight-edge pieces."

"In a way," Conte said, "we'd all be better off if she were dead."

Dennison shrugged, as if he were purely neutral on the subject. "In a way," he agreed. "Or back in our hands. But if she *is* dead, we want the corpse—or at least positive proof that she is one."

"So far," Conte said, "that isn't much to go on."

"There's more," Dennison said. "I talked to some of my old contacts in Washington, and I sent Vang to visit his CIA pal, Peter Chamberlain."

Conte nodded. Vang was patriarch of the American Hmong refugee community, and onetime commander of the Hmong mercenary forces during the Vietnam War. Before the fall of Saigon, Vang had assured his future and those of several hundred of his people by amassing documentary evidence of the CIA's involvement in the Southeast Asian heroin trade. Peter Chamberlain had been his control, and it was to Chamberlain that Vang brought the evidence and his

demands. The man who was now a senior agent was the
perfect choice, although he himself was honest and had
nothing to do with the drug traffic. But Chamberlain loved
the agency, and by threatening to drag its name in the mud,
Vang was frequently able to manipulate Chamberlain into
providing information and helping in other ways.

"Chamberlain and the others," Dennison said, "confirmed that Dana was a free lance, selling to all comers. At
the time of his murder his known clients were a privately
held Japanese microchip manufacturer and a Russian KGB
field agent stationed in San Francisco. The FBI is supposed
to handle domestic operations, and it turns out that in this
case they did. In fact, they knew about Dana's shenanigans
almost from the beginning, but they decided to allow him to
operate—and to use him as a conduit of disinformation."

The waitress came over, and Miss Paradise ordered
another piña colada, "no parasol."

"A major American electronics firm was cooperating
in regard to Dana's Japanese client," Dennison went on.
"They were real happy to make life more difficult for a
foreign competitor. One of their junior executives posed as a
computer thief and passed outdated or outrightly incorrect
technical information to Dana, for retransmittal to his
Oriental client. The KGB man was played the same way;
he's young, inexperienced, and not very smart. Anyway, the
setup worked so well that the bureau decided to let Dana
continue to operate. It was a good idea, except they made
one mistake." Dennison smiled faintly. "It happens."

"Yeah," Miss Paradise said. "Except with the FBI it
happens about once a week." She looked at Conte. "Give
me back my parasol."

Dennison watched Conte hand it over. "You can't
expect the bureau to get the job done like we do," he said.
"They're supposed to play by the rules."

"Which is why we operate like we do, right, boss dear? Someone has to keep the world safe for democracy."

"We get the job done," Dennison said, and showed her his smile. "But you're right about the bureau. It's basic tradecraft that if you're running a drone agent, you maintain twenty-four-hour surveillance. The FBI didn't play it that way. They were keeping tabs on Dana's operation, but not on his personal life."

"So they didn't know he was playing around with Melinda Bannister," Conte guessed.

"They found out twelve days ago," Dennison confirmed, "one day *after* the two of them slipped out of the country." Dennison leaned back in his chair. "That's where we run out of hard facts."

Over Miss Paradise's bare shoulder Conte saw Mabel Jones's statuesque figure come out of the bar onto the patio. She looked around and smiled broadly when she spotted him, then cut a straight trail to the table, yodeling, "There you are."

Dennison rose gracefully, and Conte, taken a little by surprise, followed suit. When he introduced Dennison and Miss Paradise, Mabel Jones shook each of their hands in turn. Miss Paradise watched the handsome older woman with evident amusement, and Conte could see that she liked her right off. Usually she kept her distance from other women.

"Aren't you going to offer that drink you owe me?" Mabel Jones asked.

Conte felt himself color. "I . . ."

"Don't say it," Mabel Jones interrupted. "I can recognize a private *tête-à-tête* when I see one, and I'm not offended." With some relief Conte could see she was telling the truth; her midwestern good humor seemed intact. "But if I don't get my drink when you all are finished," she went on, staring at Conte, "you will be sorrier than a three-legged heifer." With that parting shot Mabel Jones skated back into the bar.

Miss Paradise was watching him with great good humor as Conte sat down. He took out a cigarette and lit it and blew smoke in her direction, then pointed a finger and said, "One word out of you, and you are in big trouble."

Dennison laughed. "She'll be a handful, Matt. Don't turn your back on her."

Conte sighed. "I thought you were on my side, Dennison."

"I am. That's why we better wrap this up. It'll give you a head start." His smile faded. "The rest of what Miss Paradise and I have put together is speculation, so if any of it sounds shaky to you, speak up. We do know that soon after Dana met Melinda Bannister in a disco and found out who she was and what she was worth, he offered her a lot of cash for information—and she turned him down flat. She may be a lousy judge of character, but her security record is clean, and she probably isn't a traitor."

"You can make a traitor out of anyone," Conte said flatly. "Either you give them a lot of what they want, like money, or a lot of what they don't want, like pain."

"Then why didn't she dump Dana as soon as he popped the question? She was supposed to be so brilliant: didn't she have the brains to know she had a good chance of looking real bad?"

"Apparently not. She liked to take chances; for all we know, she may be missing the bull's-eye by a couple of rings. She had pulled the play before, and Dana fit her idea of a thrill."

"She could have even loved him," Miss Paradise put in. She nodded in the direction in which Mabel Jones had departed. "You never can tell what'll attract people."

Conte ignored the bait. "Did Dana love her?"

Dennison pursed his lips. "Hard to say. He was probably attracted to her."

"Probably," Miss Paradise repeated sarcastically. She clicked open the clasp of her page and took out a tissue-paper envelope, which she tossed in front of Conte. Inside was a single 3 × 5 color photograph.

Melinda Bannister was dressed for tennis, and the effect would not have been more erotic had she been nude. Her blond hair was hanging down in two braids, and she wore a visor made of green-tinted celluloid. The tails of the man's shirt she wore were tied under her breasts, and all of the buttons were undone. Her shorts were of some sort of thin satiny material and slit up the side, and she wore white knee socks and low-cut tennis shoes.

"What do you think, Conte?" Miss Paradise said. "Do you think Dana was attracted to her?"

"It's a fair shot," Conte said. "Dana sounds like a creep, but he doesn't sound crazy."

"But he also wanted to use her," Dennison said. "He tried it when they met, and there is no reason to assume he gave up the idea. Either he was somehow milking her already, or he was hedging with her against the future."

"Poor guy," Miss Paradise said, "having to take his work home with him like that."

"Which kept the FBI from getting wind of the scheme," Conte pointed out. "Dana had some brains after all."

"Yeah, and now they're decorating the sand at Monte Carlo."

"Colorfully put, my dear," Dennison said. He finished what was left of his highball and set the glass aside. "My guess is that Dana took Melinda Bannister to Europe with one of two things in mind. We know he had contacts among the terrorist community, and he may have meant to hire a couple of their people to soften her up for interrogation."

"Maybe."

"Or he meant to sell her outright."

Conte nodded. "That makes more sense."

"In either case, she thought they were just taking a vacation, and she went with him with free will."

"If you say so." Conte crushed out his cigarette. "Why do you think he was killed?"

"It might have nothing to do with Melinda Bannister. Dana could have double-crossed someone on some other deal—he was playing in the big leagues—or he may have made an enemy. It could even have been an accident. In which case they killed the woman, too, or snatched her because they thought they could use her. Caucasian women fetch a good price on the other side of the Mediterranean."

"But that's not what you think happened," Conte suggested.

"No," Dennison said. "I think the killer knew who Melinda Bannister was, in terms of dollars or gold, and killed Dana to take her away from him."

Dennison looked across the pool to the ocean. The tide was in, and the moon played highlights across the waves' froth. "You've got to find her, Matt, and bring her back— dead or alive."

"Which means finding Dana's killer."

Dennison nodded.

"I hate to be a pessimist, Dennison, but right there is the hard part."

"I have one more source to contact, Matt, and I think he's going to help us out on that part. If he can, will you take the job?"

"The usual fee?"

"One hundred thousand bucks, Conte," Miss Paradise said. "Enough to finance your wastrel life-style for two, maybe three months. It's a good thing you don't drink."

"I make up for it with my other vices." He nodded to Dennison. "I guess you're on. I can't have any worse luck than I was having at the tables."

Dennison stood, and again Conte was struck with the contrast between Dennison's almost stocky appearance and the effortless agility of his physical movements. "Fine, Matt. That's just fine." Dennison was beaming now like a father whose son had just handed over an all-A's report card. He offered his hand and Conte shook it.

Dennison grinned at Miss Paradise and nodded toward the cocktail lounge. "We're in the way, my dear." He stood.

Conte looked over his shoulder and saw Mabel Jones hovering near the bar. "Anyway," Dennison went on, "it doesn't look like you'll need us to keep you company for the rest of the night."

"Go to town, Hot Shot," Miss Paradise said. But when she came around the table she stopped to brush his cheek with her lips, and murmur in his ear with absolute sincerity, "Good luck, Matt. I'll tell Chris you asked for her." Conte could not have been more surprised if she had announced she was carrying his child, and all he could do was stare stupidly at their backs as they disappeared into the cocktail lounge's dimness.

They were gone by the time he followed, but Mabel Jones was still there, ready, willing, and—as Conte found out two drinks later—more than able.

Chapter Two

"You'll like George Petrie, my dear," Dennison said.

"Like I always say, boss dear, any spy of yours is a spy of mine."

"Oh, George was not your average workaday spy, my dear. He was tops, aces, the crème de la crème."

"Even if he was KGB."

Dennison looked at her. "You've been going through the personnel files again."

"That's what you pay me for, boss. I've got to keep on top of things."

"To make sure I don't do anything you wouldn't do," Dennison pointed out. "What you're really keeping on top of is me."

Miss Paradise slid her bottom closer to his and took his right arm in both her hands. "Gee, boss," she murmured, "I love it when you talk dirty."

The taxi jerked to a stop for a red light at Forty-sixth Street. It was lunchtime, and the sidewalk on Fifth Avenue seemed to be teeming with young women, and to Dennison's eye every one of them was wonderfully lovely. He wondered if age made the eye more forgiving. "The Girls in Their Summer Dresses"; the phrase leaped into his mind. He wondered where it came from.

"Irwin Shaw," Miss Paradise said. "The title of one of his short stories."

Dennison looked at her narrowly. "Very impressive,

my dear. I know we've grown close during these my twilight years, but I didn't know you could read my mind."

"You were talking to yourself, boss dear." She took his hand, as the cab pulled forward with a quick squeal of rubber.

Dennison shook off his reverie. "I should have guessed from the duds that you'd checked up on old George." She was wearing a white peasant blouse with a deep scoop neckline, a full cotton skirt in a flower print, a matching babushka, and sandals.

At the next one-way street the cab cut right toward Park Avenue, veering hard enough to throw Miss Paradise almost into Dennison's lap. "George was a deputy assisant director at the end, you know," he said when they were untangled. "He was a Party member. His name was Gregor Petrov in those days, of course, but don't call him by that now. He gets a big kick out of the idea of being an American."

"Yeah," Miss Paradise said. "So do I."

"George was six months from his pension when they arrested him," Dennison went on. "He was charged with 'activity detrimental to the Soviet cause,' whatever the hell that means. He never learned who had made up the lies about him, so one of his hobbies is investigating the frame-up. Anyway, he was convicted and sent to a prison camp in Yakut for 'reeducation.'"

Miss Paradise snuggled closer and shuddered. "Just thinking about it makes me cold."

"It has the same effect on George. He wears a sweater year-round, even when everyone else is giving off steam."

The cab driver had hit a lick with the lights and was weaving in and out of traffic at about 40 miles per hour. "Seventeen months later he was released, and they didn't say any more than when they took him in. But George didn't care about reasons; he just defected the next time he got out of the country.

"Now," Dennison said, "this part you'll really like: after the CIA debriefed George, he asked them for a job. During the two decades he spent on the other side of the game, he'd worked up an international network of informers and contacts. Of course every agent does something like that—but no one as well as George. But the agency took him for an old geezer who was ready for the glue factory. They wrote him up for a hundred-and-fifty-dollar-per-month retainer, patted him on the head, and told him, 'Don't call us, we'll call you.'"

"That sounds like the agency, all right."

"So George went free-lance," Dennison pressed on. "He still has his network, and he still uses it to run a sort of information bureau."

"Which is why we're here."

"Right," Dennison said. "Oh, yeah," he went on. "I almost forgot to tell you: George isn't calling himself a spy anymore. He's only in it for the money, until he can make a go of his true profession."

"I'll bite."

Dennison looked at her and said solemnly, "He wants to be a writer."

Twenty blocks further uptown in an apartment in the East Eighties, George Petrie sat at his kitchen table, hunched over a battered fifteen-year-old Smith-Corona manual typewriter. The apartment was pleasant by New York City standards, but certainly not luxurious; what Petrie liked best about it was that the park was only a block and a half distant. He had sparse, close-cropped gray hair and a stoop, and wore baggy wool trousers with pleats in front, a white shirt and dark tie, and a cardigan that buttoned up the front. Although it was nearly eighty degrees in the apartment, and somewhat muggy, the air-conditioning was off. In fact, it had not been turned on since a day six years earlier on which fourteen Manhattanites had died of heart attacks directly attributed to the heat.

Petrie cranked a sheet of paper out of the little typewriter, adjusted wire-rimmed bifocals, and read what he had written:

Chapter Forty-one
Khrushchev and Malenkov: The Best of Both Worlds

In the middle of the 1950s, when Khrushchev was unseating Malenkov in my country, and American general Eisenhower was unseating Stevenson in yours, it was halcyon days for the Soviet spy. This was the Cold War, and nobody trusted anybody. The Americans did not trust the Russians, the Russians did not trust the Americans, the Russians did not trust the other Russians, and nobody trusted the Germans. But nobody ever trusted the Germans.

I myself was in London in those days, spying upon the British. The British were civilized about spying, and liked to swap tales over tea. I also like to drink tea, so that was fine. I would swap tales with a British spy named Marlowe, tales of nothing so startling, but it gave us each something to take back to our Controls. The only two things that I did not like about England were the weather and the women. Both were chilly, it seemed to me.

Petrie placed the sheet facedown on top of a stack perhaps four inches thick. This was the manuscript of his memoir, entitled *My Twenty Years with the KGB*. Petrie had been working on it for seven years and expected to finish any time now. He had been lately telling friends that he "could see the light at the end of the tunnel." It was one of his favorite American phrases.

Petrie had a lot of friends, because he was a genuinely likable man who liked other people. So when he heard the knock on the apartment door he rose quickly and had to stop himself from going to answer. Yetta liked to do the door answering and complained when he interfered. Yetta liked to complain, though she was really quite a happy woman. With her it was a way of passing the time, like knitting.

"So?" Petrie heard Yetta say. "*Nu?*" A moment later she led Dennison and Miss Paradise into the room.

Petrie glowed with his pleasure. "My friend," he said warmly, and took Dennison's right hand in both of his. He had to stand on tiptoes to reach Miss Paradise's cheek with his lips.

"Can we talk, George?" Dennison said.

"I know what that means, 'can we talk?'" Yetta Plant said behind him. She was a huggably soft woman of perhaps fifty, with hair the color of crepe-paper flames. She and George had been living together for six and a half of the seven years since he had defected. She liked to complain about his sweaters, his snoring, and the fact that he refused to marry her until he was a published author, and "could support her like she deserved."

"It means," Yetta Plant complained, "you three go somewhere and talk and leave me all alone. Even you"— she gestured impatiently at Miss Paradise—"you gorgeous big girl, you don't stay and talk to me, like girls should. There are things I could tell you, girl."

"I know you could, Yetta," Miss Paradise said, soothingly as she was able.

"Tea first," Yetta announced. "Then you run off and do whatever it is you think is so important that old women cannot listen to it."

Yetta served the tea in tall glasses with thick wedges of lemon stuck to the bottom by long-handled spoons, and sugar cubes to be held between the back teeth while drinking. "You're looking fit, Yetta," Dennison said around his sugar cube.

Yetta Plant beamed with pleasure at the compliment and complained, "I am a fat old woman with no time for your flattery." She pointed an accusing finger at Dennison, cocking her head at the same time in Miss Paradise's direction. "Why don't you feed this girl, Dennison? Look at how skinny she is, nothing but hair and flesh and bones. You must be sick, sweetheart, with this man not feeding you."

"Yetta," Petrie murmured.

Yetta planted her tea on the table and threw up both hands in a gesture of defeat. "Go," she said, in the tones of a great martyr. "Go and do your talking that is so secret, not for old women's ears."

But as they were leaving the apartment, Yetta caught Miss Paradise by the arm. "Don't listen to what I said," she whispered, but loud enough to be sure Dennison could hear. "You look very beautiful, but I don't want *him*"—she cocked her head contemptuously—"to take you for granted. They will you know, if you let them. Look at George."

Down on the street it was the best kind of New York City summer day, Dennison thought. The air had hardly any taste at all, the sky was cloudless and the sun warm, and the humidity was nowhere near high enough to wilt his seersucker sports jacket. Children played games on the stoops of brownstones, and in front of an apartment building two girls were chalking a hopscotch grid on the narrow sidewalk. The people they passed were as handsome as the ones downtown, and Dennison wondered if New York was enjoying a renaissance, or if it was only the benign presence of George Petrie, which seemed to color everything.

They crossed the avenue to the park, pausing for a moment to let a herd of a dozen women in bright halters and T-shirts and flimsy shirts jog past. A man and a woman, both in business suits, had spread a blanket on the grass and were having a picnic lunch from a wicker basket, and a little further on two young men without shirts were tossing a Frisbee back and forth, while an indefatigable German shepherd raced between them, following the Frisbee's flight.

Everything seemed to Dennison serene and pleasant and calming, as if George Petrie were acting on him like a mildly euphoric drug. He almost hated to bring up business—especially the business of death—for fear it would puncture the tranquility like a tack in a tire.

But George Petrie seemed to sense his mood, because he brought up the subject himself. "Have you ever heard the name Vancouver?" he asked. "A man, not a place."

"I don't think so," Dennison said.

But Miss Paradise said, "It's come up as a cross-reference in the files. Just a name so far; nothing's been correlated."

Petrie held up a forefinger. "True, dear girl—until recently."

They stopped in front of a bench under the shade of a maple, and Petrie bowed slightly and gestured palm-up, like a gracious host. "Vancouver is a man of blood," he said as they sat. "He is a mercenary assassin who will go anywhere for anyone who can pay his fee." Petrie's tone was as matter-of-fact as if he were discussing an automobile mechanic. "He appears to have neither nationality, politics, nor history, although there is some belief that he came out of the Vietnam conflict."

"Which side?"

Petrie shook his head. "There is talk both ways." A couple strolled by the bench, a young man in a twill sports jacket with handkerchief in the breast pocket, navy slacks, slip-on shoes with buckles on the front, and a rep tie; and a woman in khaki Bermuda shorts, a white blouse that showed off a weekends-at-the-shore tan, and cross-strap sandals. The woman's arm was around the man's waist, and as they passed she looked up and said something Dennison did not hear. The man laughed easily, not for her benefit but from genuine good humor and pleasure, and Dennison found himself daydreaming again: a young executive of some sort meeting his wife for a lunch-hour walk, handsome prosperous people with a summer place on the Island and no worries beyond Friday-afternoon commuter traffic, and then the sun setting where the ocean touched the sky, backlighting other couples just as handsome, and the smell of grilled steaks and barbecue smoke.

"This much is certain," Petrie said. "Vancouver is extremely good, extremely lethal—perhaps the best in all the world."

"Boss dear," Miss Paradise said softly.

Dennison shook his head. "I'm listening." But he saw her look of concern, and wondered himself why he seemed to suddenly be avoiding the situation. Part of it was the incongruity, this talk of the most violent and impersonal sort of death in the middle of this cityscape of thriving life. But another part was that Dennison had had a hunch it would devolve into something like this. As deadly a killer as they had ever gone up against—this is what he would be sending Matt Conte into—and it was a damned good bet that only one of them, Conte or Vancouver, would live through the confrontation.

"How much?" Dennison said.

"I beg your pardon, old friend."

"Vancouver's fee."

Petrie sighed. "One half million dollars."

"Damn," Miss Paradise breathed.

"For that amount of money," Petrie went on, "Vancouver only accepts the most dangerous jobs, because those are the jobs of greatest value to his clients. One does not pay five hundred thousand dollars to have one's nagging wife buried under the lilacs." Petrie smiled vaguely. "He advertises, of a sort. He has trademarks. He uses a .22-caliber weapon for a single head shot. He employs a silencer for both discretionary purposes and to cause diversionary disruptions if his victim is among other people."

"Sure," Miss Paradise nodded. "Someone suddenly goes down with a hole in his head, without any sound of gunfire, and people are apt to get a little wound up."

It fit the way Andrew V. Dana had been taken out on the Monte Carlo beach, Dennison noted. "What are his credits?" he asked.

"What you would expect," Petrie said. "The first verifiable kill was the progressive head of a small African state, which was soon after overthrown by a repressive military coup. Some time after that a British MP was ostensibly killed in the explosion of a rigged automobile in a London mews, but the autopsy revealed he had been shot in the head first; the provisional wing of the IRA claimed credit, but it is now assumed to have been Vancouver's work. There was an aggressive and very hawkish Israeli army general named Yitzhak Rabim upon whom the PFLP had put a large bounty, and most recently an American financier named Alvin Dortmund, who had reputed links to your Mafia and was scheduled to testify in the racketeering trial of a Chicago union leader."

"This Vancouver gets around," Miss Paradise said.

"So it would appear."

"Where is his home base?" Dennison asked.

"No one knows?"

Dennison frowned. "No ideas whatsoever? No one in your network has heard any rumors, George?"

Petrie held out both hands, as if delivering a benediction. "Between assignments, my friend, Vancouver does not exist. There are no photographs of him, not even a verbal description. Vancouver materializes, and someone dies with a bullet in his head—and Vancouver is gone like mist."

"Age?"

Again Petrie shook his head no. "His work dates from the mid-seventies—that may be the origin of the rumor that he was involved somehow in the war. Beyond that nothing of him is known."

There was a racket of clicking wheels, and Dennison looked up to see a young woman roller-skating down the sidewalk toward them. She was about twenty, with straight blond hair and a golden tan, wearing jogging shorts over a clinging leotard top: a tiny bit of southern California teleported to Central Park. She skated stiff-legged, awkward as a child, and she almost lost her balance when she came to a circling stop in front of him.

"Hi, Mr. Petrie," she said, slightly out of breath. Petrie began to rise, but she said, "Hey, wow, don't get up."

Petrie made introductions, evidently pleased at the

woman's attention. Dennison thought it must have to do with the time Petrie had spent in the Siberian jail; the deprivation of any real human company must have strengthened his regard for his fellows. Dennison found himself vaguely envious: the commonplace had become precious for George Petrie, and always would be. He watched the girl's lithe figure as she skated away.

"How do you contact Vancouver?" Dennison pulled his gaze reluctantly from the girl and regarded Petrie again. "Let's say you want to buy him, for example."

"He's in a dicey position," Miss Paradise said, thinking aloud. "He's left enough corpses in his wake to have pissed off some powerful people. He's got the kind of enemies you want to keep a goodly distance from. But at the same time he has to be accessible to people who want to hire him."

"Exactly," Petrie beamed. "And I think you'll be impessed by Vancouver's solution. He has let it be known among those who might wish to employ him—organized international crime, the terrorist network, those areas of the Third World where revolution is a national sport—how he can be reached. Each day at noon, Greenwich mean time, he monitors a certain radio frequency. If you wish to make contact, you are supposed to broadcast a 440-cycle tone for twenty seconds, followed by your message—it is up to you how to code it, but if Vancouver either does not understand it or does not like the purport, that is the end of it. If he does decide he wishes to know more about the proposed assignment, he will broadcast the same tone two hours later, followed by a time, date, and place at which you are to appear—alone, of course. If you follow instructions, and if Vancouver is satisfied with your behavior thus far, there is face-to-face contact to discuss details, terms, and so forth."

"With Vancouver himself?"

"Apparently he sends a representative of some sort."

"It might be possible to backtrack to Vancouver through his man," Miss Paradise suggested.

"It might. But you can safely assume that Vancouver has done whatever possible to assure against that contingency as well."

"He sounds like a planner, all right."

And a very dangerous man, Dennison thought.

"I do not ask what you want with this Vancouver, my friend," Petrie said softly. He was watching the antics of a squirrel among the branches of the maple. "I will tell you this—in the most deadly game that can be played, he has won match after match without a loss. He has survived at his business for many years for one reason: he has made no mistakes. You yourself, and your people, have also fought hard and well for many years, but never against such an opponent as Vancouver. He knows every trick that you do. To decoy him, or to lead him into a trap, will be difficult even for you, my friend."

The blond girl came skating past again, all flailing arms and long, golden legs, waving and laughing as she went by the bench.

"To kill him," Petrie said, "—and that is what you will have to do, don't you think?—to kill him will be the most difficult of all."

Petrie stood, almost abruptly. "Enough of this. The day is too fine to dwell on death for so long. You'll come back for another cup of tea?"

"Sorry," Dennison said.

"Yetta will complain," Petrie said, "and the brunt of it will fall on my head." He sighed. "But it will give her pleasure, and after all, what is love but the giving of pleasure?"

They shook hands, and again Petrie rose on his toes to

kiss Miss Paradise's cheek. Dennison watched him cross the street, a middle-aged, stoop-shouldered man who still managed to move with a spring in his step that could only come from a love of life. He should have been a grandfather a dozen times over, dawdling toddlers on his knee instead of juggling a network that reached into every sordid corner of a violent world.

Petrie's hunch was almost surely correct: if this mission was to reach a successful end, Vancouver must die along the way. All of his instinct told Dennison that Melinda Bannister's deliverance depended on Vancouver's demise.

In the balance lay more death—perhaps hundreds or even thousands of deaths—if the information in the Bannister woman's head got into the wrong hands.

Vancouver was only a man. There was nothing supernatural to him, nothing invulnerable. His flesh and bone and muscles were only that, fragile bits of living matter that would tear and shatter and bleed under the bullet's impact, as the matter that had been his victims.

But all of that also applied to Matthew Conte.

"Time to go, boss," Miss Paradise said.

She was already waving down a cab, and Dennison had time for only a quick last glance before it pulled to the curb. But it was enough. To his eyes the sunshine had dimmed a half hour earlier.

BOOK TWO

Conte's Run

Chapter Three

The moon had set two hours earlier, and since then clouds had drifted in to partially obscure the stars, so the soccer stadium was shrouded in shadow, like a veteran's coffin draped in black crepe. It was a few minutes before three in the morning, and the empty arena seemed immense, a gigantic concrete bowl sunk into the earth as if it had settled from its own sheer mass. Empty of the tens of thousands of screaming rabid football enthusiasts who normally filled it, the stadium seemed alien, otherworldly and foreboding.

Matthew Conte crouched behind the last tier of benches at one end of the bowl's oval, at least two hundred feet above the grassy field and a good quarter mile from the other end. The summer night was brisk; a stiff breeze had come up with the clouds, chill enough so Conte turned up the collar of his windbreaker. His position overlooked the full expanse of the stadium, though he knew it would take long minutes to move to another position without breaking cover. But that couldn't be helped, not without bringing in an army of men—and that was the best way he could think of to keep Vancouver from climbing out of his hole.

A cloud eclipsed the stars, and deeper blackness crept over the field. It was a savvy choice for a meet, Conte reckoned, isolated and urban at the same time, private and open-spaced—and far too many accesses to rig for an ambush. He wondered if Vancouver had used it before, and guessed not; good as the place was, Vancouver would probably go way out of his way to keep from establishing patterns.

Conte knew the drill; for one thing, he had been in a similar way of business for ten years. He grinned sourly in the darkness, thinking, *It takes a thief . . .*

He wanted a cigarette, but not badly enough to chance the light. Instead he checked the luminous dial of his Rolex—it was 2:58 A.M.—then raised the monocular in his leather-gloved right hand and scanned the field once more. The Litton Night-Vision Scope was about the size of a snub-nosed .38 revolver, but it cost about fifty times as much, and at this point was that much more useful to Conte. Using a battery-powered microprocessor called a passive light amplifier, it magnified ambient light up to five hundred times. Despite the clouds, the stadium looked bright as day to Conte. An automatic gain control guarded against any sudden blinding flashes of artificial light, and the scope was fitted with a 105 mm zoom lens variable from .7x to 4x.

Conte used both hands to hold the scope steady. In its frame was the back of a man, standing motionless in the exact middle of the soccer field's center stripe; from Conte's vantage point he looked slight and insignificant and vulnerable. He was all of that, and more.

He was a dead man if the plan went queer, or if Conte made a slow move or a poor judgment.

Conte looked over the rest of the stadium and saw only concrete and wooden pews and high-arched entry portals. Down on the field the dugout tunnels that led to the locker rooms in the structure's bowls gaped empty and silent, like the mouth of an idiot mute. Atop the side of the oval to Conte's left, a press box perched above the upper rows of seats, looking rickety and precarious on stiltlike steel latticework. He scanned the length of the building's open window, looking for the black snout of a sniper's gun, the faintest glimmer of a cigarette tip, or starlight on optical glass.

He saw nothing to interrupt the stolid inanimateness of the massive concrete saucer, nothing to indicate he and the man on the field were not alone in this unsettling universe. He clicked the magnification down to .7x for maximum scope of vision and focused on the other man's back again.

The man's name was Jonathan Kay, and the word Conte had gotten was that he was good. He'd better be, Conte thought now, covering him with the scope. He'd better be good as gold.

Europe was Dennison's idea; instinct told him the transmission should originate there. Conte had spoken to him the last time from a booth in Kennedy International Airport, listening carefully to the last-minute intelligence on the mysterious assassin known as Vancouver, jotting down a few notes on the back of an envelope. Then Dennison had given him a name—George Petrie—and a Manhattan phone number. Conte dialed it, and a pleasant-sounding man with a Slavic accent gave him a second name and a room number in the Hotel Continental on the Via Vittorio Veneto in Rome.

After he hung up, Conte went into the men's room. He studied the name and number for a few seconds, then tore up the envelope and flushed it.

Eight hours later Conte was walking under the shade of the plane trees that lined the Via Vittorio Veneto. It was seven in the morning Rome time, but the day promised to be a warm one. Conte passed a sidewalk café where half a dozen people were taking an early breakfast, costumed like extras in the decadence-of-the-bourgeoisie scene in a Fellini movie. Conte continued by an American Express office and through the lobby of the Hotel Continental, passing a great

deal of leather and marble on the way to the elevator. The
operator was a gnarled little gnome who had to be at least
eighty; cranking the old-fashioned wheel was obviously
such exertion that Conte had to restrain himself from
pitching in.

Conte rapped on the room's door twice, then twice
more, and immediately a muffled voice said, "Yes?"

"The name is Albert," Conte said.

The man who opened the door was hardly what Conte
expected. He was very young, twenty-five years old at the
outside, small framed, thin, delicate featured, almost
epicene; although he was about Conte's height he must have
weighed forty pounds less. He had fine blond hair parted in
the middle and combed straight back, and he wore a silk
shirt with the top three buttons undone to show a heavy gold
chain around his neck. There was a Patek Philippe watch
with a gold band on his left wrist, and a gold signet ring on
the fourth finger of his right hand. Conte's first instinct was
that the guy belonged down at the sidewalk café with the
rest of the Hollywood cowboys. But he had come well-
recommended. . . .

Conte went past him into the hotel suite. There was a
sitting room and a separate bedroom opening off it, but no
luggage. In fact, there was no sign the room was occupied,
with the exception of a tray on the sideboard holding an ice
bucket in which a wine bottle was buried, and two glasses.
Conte opened the closets and found them empty of either
clothes or trouble. The curtains were drawn; when he pulled
them aside he could see at the end of the Via, the Villa
Borghese and the park that surrounded it.

"Did you check under the bed?" the thin man said.

Conte regarded him. The thin man shut the door and
went to the sideboard. "A glass of wine?"

"No thanks."

The young man poured, then took a gold cigarette case from his pocket and offered it. Conte shook his head and got out one of his own.

"You are a friend of George Petrie?" The young man had a vague and unidentifiable accent.

"No."

The young man smiled politely.

"George Petrie is a friend of a friend of mine. There's something I have to take care of, but I can't pull it off alone. George Petrie told my friend you could handle the job." Conte blew out smoke. "I'm not so sure."

The young man uncorked the wine bottle and half-filled one glass. Conte noticed the bottle was already down one-third. The young man sat in a velvet-upholstered armchair with curved oak arms and legs. Conte remained standing.

"You know, Albert, people's tendency to jump to conclusions never fails to fascinate me." His tone was still casual, but now it had a slightly hard edge. "Stereotypes are so much more easy to assimilate; they are known quantities and as such they do not threaten. For example: a person observes a man of slight build and certain gestures, wearing jewelry perhaps, and sometimes that person will leap to a conjecture."

The young man drained the last of the wine from his glass—and then his hand moved, quick as thought. The glass flipped end-over-end in a lazy arc at Conte. Automatically he reached out a hand and caught it, right side up—and froze.

The young man was holding an ugly little .22 automatic on him.

The snout was no wider than a drinking straw, the entire gun no bigger than a cigarette pack. It had an effective range of maybe twenty feet tops, and even then the slug would have to be precisely aimed to do any real damage.

All that passed through Conte's mind—along with the sudden moral certainty that the young man needed no more gun than the .22 to put Conte's lights out for good.

"For my business," the young man said in the same pleasant conversational tone, "it's sometimes an advantage to mislead people." He smiled and hefted the little gun on his palm. "And appearances *can* be deceiving, don't you think?"

"What is your business?"

"Assisting people in *your* business, my friend."

Conte reached inside his sports coat, moving carefully. The other man watched him; the little gun still lay flat on his palm. Conte drew out a white letter-sized envelope and flipped it at the other man like a playing card. The other man caught it without taking his eyes from Conte. The guy was right, Conte had to admit to himself: he had jumped to some wrong ideas.

The other man peered inside the envelope and said, "Ah." It contained $20,000 in American currency. He lay the .22 carelessly on the sideboard behind him. "Thank you, Albert."

"The hell with this cloak-and-dagger stuff," Conte said. "The name is Matt Conte."

"Jonathan Kay," the young man said, almost gravely. "You understand, Mr. Conte—"

"Matt."

"—Matt . . . I had to see to some degree how you behave under stress. Whatever you want me to do involves, I imagine, some danger." He waved the envelope. "About twenty thousand dollars' worth, is my guess. I might be putting my life in your hands."

Conte straightened from where he was leaning against

the hotel room wall. "Now that you mention it," he said, "you are."

Jonathan Kay had listened carefully to Conte's instructions. When Conte finished, Kay extended his right hand palm-down, spread his fingers, and carefully examined his own immaculately manicured fingernails before saying, "*If* I am able to make the radio call, and *if* there is a response, and *if*—"

"I get it," Conte interrupted. "You reckon there are a lot of ifs. What's the point?"

"Why do you want to make contact with Vancouver?"

Conte shook his head.

"I'd like an idea of what I'm getting into."

Conte looked at his watch; it was almost eight local time, an hour earlier GMT. "I'll give you one in seven hours, providing you make contact."

That seemed to satisfy Kay. He had one more glass of wine, then went out. Conte had breakfast in the hotel café; the eggs were watery and the rolls soggy, but the coffee was espresso, hot and thick and strong as kerosene. Back in the room he stood at the window and smoked and looked north over Rome, not thinking about anything at all. He had dozed fitfully on the plane, and when he lay down on the unruffled bed he fell asleep almost immediately.

He awoke to the scratching of a key in the doorlock. He sat up quickly, glanced at his watch—3:10 P.M.—and then rested his hand under his jacket on the butt of the .45 automatic he wore there.

Jonathan Kay went directly to the sideboard. He poured what was left of the wine into a glass and got a cigarette lit before looking at Conte.

"Belgrade, Yugoslavia," he said through a cloud of smoke. "Three A.M. local time, on the center stripe of the soccer stadium. One man, prepared to deliver the five-hundred-thousand-dollar fee. No backup of any kind, no second man for cover." Kay put down the wine in one neat lump, then patted at his lips with his pocket handkerchief. "You know as well as I: if they get the faintest scent of anything one tiny bit out of the ordinary, the contact man is dead as Caesar. Are you willing to take the chance?"

"I'm not the contact man," Conte said evenly. "I'm the cover."

"Ah," Kay said.

"You asked for an idea of what you were getting into."

"As the Americans say," Kay drawled, "that sucks."

"Yeah. It's a rotten world."

For a full minute, Kay gazed at Conte, his eyes hooded, half-closed. He looked disturbingly like Dennison, playing possum just before he sprung something on you. Finally Kay stood up. He took out the white envelope, unfolded it, and pursed his lips, as if he had found a turd in his pocket.

Jonathan Kay smiled almost apologetically at Conte. "Too bad," he murmured.

Then he put the envelope back in his pocket. He tossed the room key on the bed. "We'd best be going," he said softly. "I've already made reservations on the three-forty-five flight to Belgrade, and I'd hate to waste the effort."

From his position behind the top tier of seats in the Belgrade soccer stadium, Matt Conte heard the triple chime of a bell, faint yet crisp on the night air. On the field Jonathan Kay lit a cigarette, turning to one side away from the breeze, cupping the flame of his lighter in both hands.

At the other end of the stadium, at ground level, there was an eyeball-searing explosion of white light.

Despite the Litton scope's automatic gain control,

Conte shut his eyes in reaction and turned away. But when the afterimage of the starburst faded from his retinas, he was still unable to see anything past the light; in the blackness of the now fully overcast night, it seemed sharp as a laser.

It was aimed directly at Kay, like a baby spot on a torch singer. In his position, barely fifty yards from it, Kay would be effectively blinded. A deep basso voice said something that Conte could not make out, but Kay began to walk toward the beacon. He moved casually, neither too quickly nor too slowly, his hands loose but well away from his body and always in plain sight, looking like a pro.

He'd better be, if they were going to make it through the next five minutes in one piece.

Conte moved out, circling around toward the light behind the top row of seats, crouched to remain in the shadow of the retaining wall. He was working under the theory that Vancouver's contact man was alone, because it was in Vancouver's interest to keep the meet limited to as few people as possible. Also, Vancouver's choice of location, and the gag with the blinding spotlight, all made it look like a one-man setup.

It'd be hell if he was wrong.

But no one shot at Conte or called to him or otherwise interfered as he dogtrotted around the high perimeter, trying to strike a balance between speed and concealment. If he was spotted, Kay would likely be shot on the spot—but if he didn't get to him soon, Kay would be shot for an imposter anyway.

Conte was halfway around the stadium, and Kay halfway to the light, when Conte got his first glimpse of the figure behind it. He had a sense of dark massive bulk.

He made it around to the man's back before starting down the shallow steps. His legs were beginning to ache from the awkwardness of his crouch, and he had to concentrate on controlling his breathing so its noise wouldn't give him away. That made his lungs ache. The steps were too broad to be taken in single consecutive strides, and halfway down he stumbled, the side of his shoe scraping concrete with a sound that seemed louder than a gunshot. Conte dropped behind the nearest bench and used the night scope.

The guy with the light was big all right, and perhaps because he had swarthy skin and vaguely Oriental features, he reminded Conte of a sumo wrestler, barrel shaped and big stomached, but a long way from being fat. He was barefooted and bareheaded, and his skull was shaved to the scalp. The black T-shirt he wore above black jeans looked spray-painted on, every muscle in his arms and chest and back as defined as in an anatomical schematic. He stood about six and a half feet tall and could not have weighed less than three hundred pounds. The light was a carbon-arc spot mounted atop a case the size of an automobile battery.

Jonathan Kay stood within its beam, ten yards in front of the gorilla-shaped man. As Conte moved out again, he saw Kay smile slightly and shake his head, as if they were at a cocktail party and the big man had made a particularly witty *bon mot*.

The big man said, "The money," in a curiously high-pitched voice that was accented, almost lilting.

Kay spread his hands wide. "Terribly sorry," he said, "but the fact of the matter is—"

Conte pocketed the scope, uncrated the Colt .45 automatic, stood up behind the waist-high barrier separating the front row of seats from the field, and said, "Hands high as they'll go, and after that be very very still."

The big man spun fluidly, the blinding spotlight raking toward Conte's position.

Conte had been expecting that move. He drew up the

.45 in both hands and caressed the trigger. The lens and element of the carbon-arc light exploded in a spray of shattered glass, and winked out.

Beyond the big man, Jonathan Kay darted out of the line of fire. "Cover me, friend," he called. "I am blinder than a mole."

Conte had been behind the light for the better part of two minutes, and his night vision was unimpaired. But then so was the big man's.

He turned to Conte, his dark Oriental face screwed up in rage, and took a step toward him.

"Hold it," Conte ordered. The big man wasn't showing a weapon.

The big man came at him, arms loose at his side, hands crabbed into sledge-sized fists.

"Hold up, goddamn it," Conte said. Up close the man was immense, big enough to snap bones like kindling in his bare hands—and Conte was frightened. Dammit, if he killed the guy it was the end of the trail. . . .

The brown-skinned Oriental was five yards away, his hate-contorted face like something monstrous.

Conte put a slug into the grass between his feet.

The big man shook his head and snarled and came on, reaching out one massive arm.

Conte shot him in the shoulder.

The big man took a step backward and stared at Conte with something like surprise, as if gunfire was not part of the tacit bargain they had made. Then he lurched forward again.

Conte retreated an involuntary step. A .45 slug was big around as a little finger; it was supposed to knock a man down, goddammit.

The big man lunged, hands grasping for Conte's throat.

Conte could not risk firing again. He turned half away; right now running seemed like a real right move.

Then the man half fell away, and for a moment in the dimness Conte had the uncomfortable feeling the guy had grown a second head. "Jesus, Conte, give me a hand," Jonathan Kay grunted, and Conte realized the thin man had jumped the gorilla, hanging on by hands and legs like a child taking a piggyback ride.

Conte held the .45 butt-out and slammed it into the side of the swarthy man's head, stepping into the blow and putting everything he had into it, hard enough to crack a normal man's skull.

Unbalanced by Kay's weight, the big man went down backward. Kay scrambled out from under him with lithe agility.

He was almost clear when the guy grabbed his ankle. Kay yelped with pain and shock.

Conte hit him again, and the guy shook his head like a heavyweight taking a good shot and used to it. There was blood all matted in his hair and smeared across his right cheek.

The big man twisted his arm and Kay went cartwheeling into the darkness. Before the Oriental giant could fully recover, Conte hit him a third time, on the back of the head at the point of his crown. It sounded like something cracked.

The big man made it to his feet, but now he was swaying like a drunk. He lunged for Conte and missed, and Conte hit him once more, not taking the time to aim but clubbing down with the gun.

The guy went down on his stomach and twitched. He braced both arms like an exhausted athlete determined to do one last push-up, and managed to flop over on his back.

Kay came up and kicked him in the temple, the same one from which blood still flowed, and the man lay still.

Conte and Kay stood over the man, breathing raggedly into the darkness, the adrenaline rush draining out of their blood. Conte had never been involved in anything so savage, and he saw his own feelings reflected in Kay's expression: relief, but perhaps some shame as well.

They used a corroded lead pipe on the lock of one of the dressing rooms, and to their surprise, the showers worked. It took five minutes before the big man was conscious, and in that time Conte had a chance to study him. The Oriental aspect of his features was subtle, and his skin was the wrong color, too brown; Puerto Rican was Conte's guess, based on his years growing up on Manhattan streets. The gunshot wound was not serious; Conte had aimed to stun him, and the bullet had drilled a hole through the fleshy part of his upper arm, just below the shoulder.

Kay pushed past Conte. He had the little .22 in his hand. "Make sure he sees that artillery piece of yours," Kay said, "as soon as he opens his eyes." He put a palm against the guy's low forehead and pushed, and the man's slack jaws fell open. Kay shoved the short barrel of the .22 in his mouth. Conte moved around and took a bead between his eyes, from about four feet.

Kay kicked the man between the legs, not very hard. Conte looked at him with some curiosity; nothing in the hotel room had prepared him for this aspect of the thin, epicene man.

The gorilla moaned and opened his eyes. He tried to twist away from the gun in his mouth, and Kay bore down. The gorilla stopped trying to move. His eyes found Conte's .45.

"Okay," Conte said.

Kay stepped back, covering the man.

Conte was satisfied to see pain in his eyes. He reached up with the same wondrous expression Conte had seen before, rubbing at the cut at his temple, then clutching his shoulder.

"Name," Conte said to him.

The big man glared at him.

"He speaks English," Kay said evenly. "At least he did a few minutes ago."

"Name," Conte said again.

The big man shook his head.

"What I want is a name," Conte told the man. "Make one up if you like." The idea was to get him talking; a successful interrogation always began with the simple questions. "Let's have one."

Five seconds passed. Conte nodded to Kay and said, "Hurt him."

Kay smiled. In the dimness of the locker room there was something ghastly in the expression. Kay extended the .22 in both hands, aimed at the man's kneecap.

"Rook," the man grunted.

"Well now, Rook," Conte said, "there are a few things I need to know."

When it was done, all three of them were soaked with sweat, despite the night's chill. Conte could feel the grit of it between his teeth. Rook was sprawled on the floor of the shower, his arms outspread. Conte wondered if they had killed him and was working up the strength to check—when Rook's body spasmed and he rolled to one side and vomited out gallons of rusty water.

"I thought you drowned him," Conte gasped.

"So did I," Kay admitted. "The water is always tricky business."

Rook tried to sit up. His face was a grotesque mask of blood. All four of his front teeth were missing, and there was a three-inch gash on one cheek. The little finger of his right hand stuck out at a ninety-degree angle from the palm. His black pants were puddled in one corner, and his tree-trunk legs were smeared with filth and more blood. He looked at Conte and then at Kay again, and that look was more chilling than any verbal threat he could have delivered.

"He's done," Kay said tonelessly. His leg shot out and his booted foot caught the man in the face. Rook made a bubbly noise and lay down again.

Conte got out a cigarette and tried to light it, but his hand was shaking. Kay took the Zippo and did it for him.

"Sorry," Conte muttered. "I've seen some things, but . . ."

"It gets different people different ways."

"Yeah," Conte said, angry at someone. He blew out smoke. "I think he got something out, before the end."

"He did," Kay said.

Conte shot him a sharp glance. "You want my advice," he said savagely, "don't fuck around with me, not just now."

"Socorro," Kay said.

"What the hell does that mean?"

"Succor, or help—in Spanish."

"Great," Conte said nastily. "So he was crying for help."

"I don't think so," Kay said. "I think it's the name of a place. It came out when you were working on his legs, and you repeatedly asked where Vancouver was."

"Jesus Christ."

"I'd follow it up if I were you," Kay said in the same

reasonable tone. "It's all you've got." Kay cleared his throat. "What about our Mister Rook here?"

"Like you said: he's done."

Kay dropped the clip out of the .22, checked the load, reseated it, and jacked a slug into the chamber. He bent and lay the barrel against Rook's massive head.

"What are you doing?" Conte noticed his voice sounded like someone else's.

Kay shot him a questioning look. "My friend, this man alive can only be deadly trouble to you."

"Forget it."

For a long moment Kay did not move. Then, slowly, he straightened, the gun still in his hand. "May I ask— purely from curiosity—why not?" His voice was cold.

"No." There was a reason, but Conte didn't feel like laying it out, not with the broken body of Rook lying in the dirty water and blood in this ugly underground place. But Conte knew: there had to be a difference between Them and Us, some sort of civility. Conte did not know what that difference amounted to—except that it began to fade when you started killing unconscious men in cold blood. "This is your territory," he told Kay. "Give me a way to keep him on ice."

"Give me ten thousand dollars, please," Kay said, almost formally.

Conte looked at him.

"I have a business relationship with the constable of a small town in Friuli East Venezia Euganea, the north-easternmost Italian province, immediately across the border. I need the money for a rental car with a strong lock on the trunk, bribes for the border guards, and another larger bribe for the constable of that town. If the bribe is large enough, the constable will lock our friend Rook up in his jail for perhaps a week." Kay's hard gaze softened slightly. "But after that, my friend, he will come for you."

"After that it won't matter," Conte snapped. He wondered how much of the ten thousand would go to the corrupt constable and how much was Kay's commission— and thought, *the hell with it*. The guy earned his keep.

Kay did not bother to count the money.

Conte waited in the shadow of one of the stadium's entrance portals for another forty-five minutes; false dawn was starting to break when Kay came back, in a black Peugeot. Rook stirred once or twice in that time, but his eyes never opened, and it was harder wrestling him into the trunk than it had been dragging him up the stairs.

"Good-bye, my friend," Kay said, and slammed the lid closed, so for a moment Conte was not sure whom he was talking to. But when Kay offered his hand Conte shook it.

He watched the black car pull off into the fading darkness, but already there were other things on his mind.

Like where the hell "Socorro" was, and the gambler's odds that he would find Melinda Bannister before she either spilled her guts, or suffered things at the hands of Vancouver that would make Rook's evening look like a church social.

Chapter Four

To a person overflying Dennison's compound it might have looked like a private hunting lodge shared by a group of usually citybound executives or their like: someone with more money than taste. The building was angular and multifaceted, as if a dozen prismatically shaped modules had been stuck together more or less at random. The exterior was redwood shakes, stained pine trim, and tinted glass, in a design with so many nooks, niches, and odd turns that it was difficult to get a notion of the building's interior layout. It housed the offices of Dennison and Miss Paradise; a combination communications center/library/data base/armory known as the Back Room—the heart, guts, and nervous system of the headquarters; and accessible by a separate entrance around back, the living quarters of Dennison, Miss Paradise, and several spare apartments.

The front porch emphasized the rustic architecture: it was shaded by a cedar-shake canopy over several pieces of cane-and-canvas lawn furniture, and reached by three split-log steps on which the bark remained. In front of it was a small clearing, but beyond that was heavy timber, mostly lodgepole pine and blue spruce, with some quaking aspen. The forest sloped away from the building, at first gently and then more steeply; the valley bottomed out nearly two thousand feet below, where a creek flowed between steep rock walls. In the spring, when it was swollen with snow-melt runoff, the rush of the big water carried all the way up to the compound if the mountain breeze was right, but now, in the summer, the only natural sound was a faint rustle of leaves.

Behind the building the slope of the mountain to which it clung grew quickly precipitous. The tree line was five hundred feet above, and from there it was another one thousand feet to the summit up a steep crumbly granite face that ended in a rock ridge-line only as wide as a city sidewalk. A twenty-foot steelwork tower straddled it, supporting two antennas and a microwave dish mounted on remote-controlled directional rotors, the tower anchored by guy wires strung from eyebolts drilled into the solid rock.

A logging road on the opposite ridge, about ten miles distant, was the only sign of access, but in fact a six-foot wide ditch was bulldozed across it a half mile from where it left the paved highway. The mountain was steep enough, and the forest growth thick enough, to effectively bar trail-bike and horseback traffic. A backpacker with excellent stamina and some technical climbing expertise could reach the compound in four or five days during the summer; an expert-class Nordic skier might be able to make it in the winter.

Dennison preferred the helicopter, a Bell Model 222 Executive that was now parked at the edge of the clearing that fronted the porch. The open space was about fifty yards to a side, generally level and grass covered. At the far edge a ten-foot pole supported a bright orange wind sock, which now hung limp in the still mountain air. Except for a few faintly discernible deer trails, the wall of trees surrounding the cleared space was unbroken.

Near the center of the clearing, Dennison was crouched over a Toro lawnmower. The grass between him and the porch was freshly trimmed, neat as a putting green; the rest of the lawn was ankle high and scruffy looking.

Dennison unscrewed the spark plug, wiped it on a greasy rag, and looked at it critically.

Miss Paradise came out on the porch, spotted the boss, and grinned. She wore a knit bandeau, shorts, and sandals, and her pale blond hair hung down over one shoulder in a single thick, long braid. She stood arms akimbo for a moment, shook her head with cheerful exasperation, and came down the steps, all long perfect legs, graceful as a ballerina.

Dennison was scraping the threads of the spark plug against the cooling fins of the 1 ½ horsepower Briggs and Stratton engine. Nothing happened. "The points," Dennison said, without looking up. "It's got to be the points."

"I never lost confidence in you, boss dear," Miss Paradise said solemnly. "Even when everything began to go black, and I saw my life pass before my eyes, I knew you'd get that lawnmower flying again." This was the Toro's fifteenth summer—"Maybe we should have a birthday party for it," Miss Paradise had said when Dennison wheeled it out of the shed that spring—but Dennison steadfastly refused to consider replacing it. Mowing the lawn was his chore, Dennison insisted, and he'd do it as he saw fit. Miss Paradise found that vastly amusing, but she went easy on the kidding. Fixing the perpetually broken-down machine was Dennison's summer therapy, a preoccupation that got his mind off the stress of his occupation.

Which was why Miss Paradise was sorry she had to get him back to business.

"Maybe you'd better let it go for now," she said gently. "I've got the printout on Socorro."

Dennison looked at her for the first time, and his eyes widened slightly. He was constantly surprised by her breathtaking beauty; it was so impeccable it was almost otherworldly, so that he sometimes expected it to evaporate, to no longer be there the next time he looked. Above the waistband of her shorts, around her geometric naval, there were a few wisps of down, so blond they were almost invisible, soft and fine as a newborn's hair, only visible because in his crouch Dennison's face was level with her crotch. He had never noticed those hairs before, though he thought he knew every inch of her body.

Reluctantly, Dennison rose and followed her to the porch, wiping grease from his hands with a piece of rag.

"Take a seat, boss," Miss Paradise said. "I'll fetch what you need."

Dennison stretched out in a chaise, positioned so his face was shaded but the rest of him caught the sun. He wore Bermuda shorts and a pair of beat-up tennis shoes. His torso was deeply tanned, and although it usually seemed barrel-like, even chubby when he was clothed, his stomach was actually hard and flat; the only indication of age was the salt-and-pepper tint of his chest hair. His arms were short but well muscled; he looked like a middleweight contender who may have lacked range, but could take and dish out a punch.

Miss Paradise came back out with a manila folder and a highball glass of Martel Five Star brandy and soda over cracked ice. By the time she had fetched a glass of chilled white wine for herself, Dennison was engrossed in the three sheets of computer-generated data the folder contained:

DATA SCAN—KEYWORD "SOCORRO"—
NAME SORT

(1) Jerry Socorro—Mafia *caporegime,* Dolo-rosi crime family, Kansas City, Missouri. Serving second year of four-year sentence for willful and deliberate tax fraud.

(2) "Socorro"—code name used by Manuel Ramirez de Herrara during tenure as Republican

espionage agent, Spanish Civil War, d. 6/8/71 of lung cancer, Barcelona.

DATA SCAN—KEYWORD "SOCORRO"—
PLACE SORT

    (1) Town, central New Mexico, U.S.A.

    (2) Town, Texas, U.S.A., suburb of El Paso.

    (3) Village, Mexico, west coast of Baja California.

    (4) Island, Revilla Gigedo Archipelago, Pacific Ocean, six hundred miles due south of the tip of Baja California; Mexican possession.

    (5) Settlement, Brazil, in Serra dos Mosquitos mountains.

    (6) Town, Brazil, suburb of São Paulo.

    (7) Mining camp, Colombia, in Cordillera Oriental mountains.

    (8) Island, believed to be in Sulu Sea area, Philippines.

Miss Paradise had pulled her chaise out into the sun, and the top of her bandeau was rolled down a bit for maximum exposure. She held the glass of wine loosely in one hand, her head was thrown back and her eyes closed.

Dennison studied the curve of her neck. "Tell me more about this last one, the island in the Philippines."

"Can't." She did not open her eyes and nothing moved except her lips. "All the computer comes up with is the name. Apparently no one has pinned down exactly what or where this Socorro is, or whether it even definitely exists."

"That's a little hard to swallow," Dennison said. "I'd think it would be hard to lose an island nowadays."

"Not so hard, boss dear. There are seven thousand and one hundred islands in the Philippines, and over sixty-five hundred of them are smaller than one square mile. Over four thousand of those don't even have names." She opened her eyes then and sat up a little straighter. "Do you remember in 1971 when scientists discovered the Tasadays? They were a tribe of twenty-eight cave dwellers who had never encountered a person from the outside world; their way of life had remained absolutely unchanged since prehistoric times. Well, the Tasadays live on Mindanao— and that's the second largest of the islands. Now if the Tasadays could get lost on Mindanao . . ."

"Vancouver could hole up pretty safely on one of the out-islands," Dennison finished. He scanned the printout again. "I'm going to eliminate the North American Socorros because there are a lot more secure hideouts for a man like Vancouver than this country or Mexico. The three South American sites are all possibilities, but none of them are very pleasant places. You could do better if you had Vancouver's income."

"Okay, that's why you don't like those places. Why do you like the Philippines?"

"For several reasons." Dennison sipped at his drink. "The political climate there could be healthy for someone like Vancouver. Since Marcos declared martial law in 1972, he's had his share of problems—civil insurrection, domestic terrorism by some Moslem groups, and no decrease in the prevalent poverty—even though he lifted the decree in '81. Marcos has also been going out of his way to make a lot of new friends; although the Philippines ostensibly remains on good terms with the U.S., Marcos has also been making an issue out of his country's membership in the Third World, and he recently established diplomatic relations and trade with the USSR, Mainland China, several Eastern bloc countries, and Communist Vietnam—even though the Philippines fought on the U.S. side during the War."

"You could call that making new friends," Miss Paradise said, almost dreamily, "or you could call it playing both ends against the middle."

"Exactly—which is why it would be nice to have someone like Vancouver owing you a favor—an island and privacy in exchange for help if and when needed. I'm not suggesting that Vancouver is Marcos's man, but he may have worked out a deal for tacit noninterference."

"Then there's this man Rook."

Dennison smiled proudly. "Very good, my dear. Go on."

"Surprise quiz time, eh?" But Miss Paradise was pleased. "One of the more common ethnic mixes in the Philippines is the *mestizo;* there the term refers to people of mixed Chinese-Filipino heritage." She batted long lashes at Dennison. "Did I pass, boss dear?"

"With flying colors."

But there was something somber in his tone, and the pause that followed was almost awkward. "The trouble is," Miss Paradise said softly, "after all that is said, it still comes down to a hunch."

"It always does," Dennison murmured. "It's the nature of the game. But if the hunch is wrong . . ."

There was no point in finishing the sentence. If the hunch was wrong, both knew the possible consequences. The death of Melinda Bannister, or her tortured revelation of ten years' worth of top secret U.S. defense information. The chance that advance word would reach Vancouver, and Matt Conte would run into a deadly bushwhack. Or any one of a dozen other lethal possibilities.

But there were times when all the data banks and reasoning and research, and contacts from here to Timbuktu, couldn't give you an absolute answer, and that was when you fell back on instinct, years of experience, and some smart guessing.

And tried to keep the egg off your face, and the blood where it belonged.

Dennison drained his highball. "Could you contact Matt and fill him in, please, my dear?" His voice sounded hollow, even to him.

Miss Paradise stood, but instead of going to the Back Room she came around behind Dennison's lounge chair. She leaned down, put both arms around his neck, and lay her cheek against the back of his head. He could feel the warmth of her breasts against his shoulder blades.

"Vancouver has made it for at least eight years in the most dangerous business in the world," Dennison said, staring at the disabled lawnmower across the grass but seeing nothing. "He is the best."

"No." Her breath tickled at his ear.

Dennison waited.

"If he were the best," Miss Paradise said, "we wouldn't have a chance. We might as well lie down and let him walk all over us." She straightened and began to knead at the muscles of Dennison's shoulders. "But we're not going to do that because we know he can be beaten—and we know we're the ones to do the job."

"Matt . . ."

"Matt knows the territory." She sounded almost irritated, like a mother chiding a child who should have known better. "He's a big boy and he can handle himself. Listen to me, boss."

She came around the chair and knelt on one knee at Dennison's right hand. "If anyone can beat Vancouver, we're the team. None of the rest of it matters. Someone has to stop him, and when they called for volunteers, it looks like we were the only people dumb enough to take one step forward." She was smiling. "It's a dirty job, but . . ."

Dennison managed to return the smile. He took her hand. "Thanks," he said, and left it at that.

Miss Paradise drew herself to her full magnificent

height, still holding his hand. "Maybe you should lie down."

"I'm not sleepy." But Dennison let her pull him out of the chair, so that when he was standing he was very close to her.

Miss Paradise looped her arm in his. "Who said anything about sleep?" she murmured.

Chapter Five

The doctor's name was Cardoza, and as soon as he saw the sleeping giant sprawled out on the cell's cot the doctor looked at his old friend the town constable and said in a reproachful tone, "Pietro, Pietro." Pietro offered a smile and a shrug that were meant to say, *you know how it is.* When the doctor's frown did not fade, the constable opened his desk drawer and took from it an envelope and passed it to him. Cardoza rifled through the five hundred American dollars inside and put it inside his coat. He gave Pietro one last scowl, meant to say, *we both know you are getting much more than this for yourself,* and then shrugged. He and Pietro, they knew each other too well.

Cardoza set his black bag on the constable's desk and unclasped it. From one compartment he took a hypodermic syringe, from another a cork-stoppered glass vial.

"What are you going to do?" Pietro asked.

The doctor gave the constable an exasperated look. "For what did you call me here?"

"To examine him."

"So I am going to examine him."

"What is the needle for?"

"To put him to sleep."

"He is already asleep."

Cardoza thumbed in the plunger of the syringe, poked the needle through the cork, then pulled the plunger back out, watching critically as the liquid was sucked from the vial. When it was empty, he removed the needle and tapped the plunger, sending a quick spurt of colorless liquid arcing through the air. Only when this ritual was completed did he take a second and closer look at the great mass of human being on the other side of the cell's bars. He lay on his back, apparently naked under the rough woolen blanket draped over the hard mound of his chest and stomach and thighs, bare arms and legs hanging over the edges of the narrow metal-framed cot. He had the dark skin of a Moor—some kind of North African, the doctor thought—but his facial features most resembled a Chinese. Even in repose, the man seemed to radiate brutality. Part of it was his sheer size and bulk; part of it was the bruises and cuts that turned what had already been an ugly visage that much uglier; even the snuffling animal snorts that the man emitted in his semiconsciousness contributed to an overall impression of mindless savagery. He was like a dray animal: built for work and pain, knowing nothing else, and grown strong and stoic because of it.

"Yes, he is asleep," Cardoza said to Pietro, "and I am going to make certain he stays that way, at least until well after I am away from here."

"And then what?" Pietro said with some alarm.

"And then, *mi amico, buona fortúna.*" From the black bag he took an eighteen-inch length of rubber tubing. "Open the cell door, please."

Cardoza circled around warily, but the brutish man on the cot gave no sign of consciousness or even life beyond the erratic mindless snorts. He sounded like a pig in truffles, Cardoza thought. The man's left arm hung palm up. Cardoza dropped to one knee, lay the syringe carefully on the concrete floor, then twisted the rubber tubing around the huge arm, just below the biceps. He grabbed the man's wrist to hold it steady as he picked up the syringe again. He found the vein immediately, drawing a few milliliters of blood into the needle to be certain, and then carefully fed the sedative solution into the man's bloodstream.

All but a few drops had been injected when the man sat bolt upright.

Cardoza screamed and scuttled back on all fours.

The doctor ended up backed into the corner away from the bars, and he watched with awful fascination as the grotesque giant swung both legs to the floor. He stared at the needle dangling from his vein, then ripped it loose and flung it at Cardoza. It shattered against the rock wall above his head, and shards of glass sprinkled down like confetti. The man got four fingers inside the rubber tubing around his arm and snapped it like a rubber band.

"Pietro," Cardoza bleated. "Your gun, *amico*. For God's sake, use it."

The big man stood, and the blanket fell away. Through his terror, Cardoza noted the man was hung like a stallion.

The man took steps toward Cardoza, and the doctor closed his eyes and began to mumble prayer, mindless as a child at bedtime. There was a leaden thump, like a sandbag dropped from a ten-story building, and the ground under Cardoza tremored. He opened his eyes: the giant's bullet head was one foot from his drawn-up legs, his eyes staring lifelessly at the ceiling.

Cardoza needed the wall's support to make his feet, and force of will to make his legs work well enough to carry him out of the cell.

Pietro was staring at him whitely. "Are you . . . did he . . . ?" The constable shook himself, like a dog come out of water. "See here, Cardoza," he said in a tone that would have been stern if his voice were not quavering. "You must examine him."

Cardoza rummaged in his bag and took out a specimen bottle half-filled with an amber liquid that looked very much like brandy. The doctor drained it in one gulp, replaced the empty bottle, and snapped his case shut. He shook free of the constable's hand on his elbow, but he turned before going out the door.

"Constable Pietro," he said with something close to dignity. "I pronounce your prisoner healthy." The doctor hiccuped discreetly and went out into the night.

The name of the town was San Anselmo, and it and its several hundred inhabitants sat in the foothills of the Carnic Alps. There was no crime in San Anselmo, but Pietro strove to be a conscientious officer just the same. On this morning, as on every morning, his uniform was clean and carefully buttoned over his paunch, and every medal was in place; that most of them represented longevity in his fraternal order was not relevant. His boots were shined, his pillbox hat set just right to cover his bald spot, and his Lüger oiled and the holster-flap fastened in place. He was a little man and he always wore a smile, partially because he actually was an easygoing sort of chap, partially to ingratiate those he met; one never knew when money might be forthcoming.

The day promised to be sunny and mild; it never got overly warm this close to the mountains. Everything in San Anselmo seemed in order, and that was as it should be. Pietro threw back his shoulders, drew in lungfuls of clean mountain air, and showed his smile to all he passed.

His office was a stone-and-mortar building near the end of the street, and here, too, order prevailed on this morning. The battered wooden chair was pushed up to the battered wooden desk, its surface empty except for a gooseneck lamp and a blotter with an advertisement for the Bank of

Milan on the border. The wall to the left was decorated with wanted posters which were beginning to yellow with age; against the right wall was a potbellied stove, unused since the last chill of spring. To the back were two barred cages.

Then Pietro saw the hulk on the bunk in the cell to the left, and his mood soured. He had truly forgotten about this guest since the unpleasantness with his friend Dr. Cardoza the evening before; it was Pietro's nature to dwell only on the cheerful.

At the sound of his entrance, the big man sat up, the woolen blanket bunched in his lap. Pietro's eyes darted to the door, but he could see the iron bolt was firmly in place.

What had the young queer called him? Pietro's memory of Kay's arrival the day before was clouded with the thoughts of what Pietro could do with the five thousand American dollars the queer had given him. *Rook*—that was it.

"Good morning, Mr. Rook," Pietro said in English.

The swarthy giant stared at him through his dull pig eyes, immobile as a monument.

Pietro sat down at his desk and adjusted the blotter. He could feel the man's gaze as if it were burning into his flesh. He managed to stand it for perhaps twenty seconds before he had to look.

It seemed like this Rook had not even blinked.

Pietro suddenly smiled. No wonder the prisoner looked so baleful; he had not eaten since coming here. A big man such as he would need much food. Food would make him feel better, and he would not glare so.

He stood and smiled at Rook and said, "Food," and pantomimed spooning food into his mouth. From Rook's reaction the constable might as well have been speaking to the stone walls, but now the constable felt better. Here was

something to do; here was a way to relieve this awkwardness.

It was perhaps fifteen minutes later when Pietro
returned from the café carrying a tray covered with a cloth.
Under the cloth were rolls and fresh butter, and stewed
prunes with thick syrup. There was a cup and a full pot of
coffee. The only utensil was a spoon. Perhaps he was only a
village constable, but Pietro was not stupid.

Rook had still not moved, but Pietro skipped no
precaution. He did not take his eyes from the man on the
bed as he bent and slid the tray through the aperture at the
bottom of the barred door. He backed carefully away until
he bumped up against his desk.

Five minutes passed before Rook raised himself from
the cot and picked up the tray. He sat on the floor, his back
against the wall and the tray in his lap, still staring at the
constable, until the constable looked away, feeling almost
ashamed, as if he had been caught spying on his mother in
the bathtub. He studied the blotter some more, but he could
not shut out the noise of the slurps and swallows and grunts
and burps with which Rook devoured the breakfast.

Pietro was careful not to look up until he heard the
clatter of the tray being slid back through the door slot.
Rook had returned to his cot. Pietro beamed. The man had
learned his lesson; there would be no more trouble now.

"It is only a week," he said. "You understand how it
is. Maybe if we must spend this time together, we can be
friends. It is lonely to be a constable in a town such as this. I
do not often get a chance to talk to people from foreign
lands." But the constable wondered if the young queer Kay
could be wrong; if this Rook did understand English, he
gave no sign. He only stared back, his cut and bruised face a
distorted but passionless mask.

Pietro stood. "I will take the tray now. Please stay back until I have done so." He smiled. A smile always put people at ease. Even a cur could smell fear, but a smile made it all fine.

The cloth that had covered the food was balled up in one corner of the tray. Pietro kept half a glance on Rook as he bent to pick it up. The big man had devoured every morsel of food he had been served. The butter dish was licked clean, the coffee pot drained; the rolls were gone, the fruit was gone—

And the spoon was gone.

Pietro felt a jolt of terror in the center of his chest. He started to straighten, and managed to look up in time to see Rook's arm cock back.

The arm whipped forward with such speed and power that the movement was almost faster than the eye could perceive.

The chubby little constable staggered back, both hands clawing at the handle of the spoon.

Its bowl was embedded in his throat.

Blood spurted out over his hands in a great wash, and Pietro could not get a grip on the three inches of handle protruding from his flesh because the metal was slippery with his own gore. He lurched forward and his forehead bounced off the iron bars of the cell. His brain seemed to explode with such agony that he could no longer see. He gasped desperately for air and inhaled thick salty warm liquid instead.

Because his brain was also hemorrhaging from the blow to the head, it only took him fifteen seconds to drown in his own blood.

Across the little cell where he sat on the bunk, Rook smiled. He rose, tied the woolen blanket around his thick waist, and went to the bars. For a long moment he stared down at the body lying in a spreading puddle of pungent mush. Then he knelt and began to rip the once-neat uniform from the constable's corpse, searching for keys.

Chapter Six

The jeepney looked like it had been designed during someone's bad LSD flashback. The chassis had once served time as part of an American government-issue jeep, but—could it speak—would now probably be too embarrassed to admit it. Mounted on it was a small buslike body, with a little compartment for the driver up front and space for maybe half a dozen passengers in back—if they were good friends. To that point it was a utilitarian and rather ingeniously designed conveyance—but from what Matt Conte had seen since coming out of the main terminal at Manila International Airport, jeepney owner/drivers were genetically incapable of leaving well enough alone.

The body was painted a bright shade of whorehouse red, with golden yellow detailing on the bumper, the continental spare, the radiator, and the doors, but Conte had to concentrate to make out the color scheme. Every free inch of the rig was covered with ornamentation. There were mirrors everywhere—bicycle mirrors, automobile mirrors, even a Michelob beer bar-mirror fastened to the rear panel; at least fifty of them sprouted like some manic chrome garden from the jeepney's hood. On the roof, where a bus's destination sign would be, was a painted banner that read "Rock-and-Sock"; another on the front bumper said "California Jam" and a third, shaped like a scalloped shell and mounted over the radiator, proclaimed "Bee-Bop-A-Lula."

At either end of the grill were foot-high silvered statuettes of roosters, beaks crowing, combs bristling, tail feathers proudly spread. Between them were two similar-sized gilded models of horses. More horses were mounted on the roof, always looking forward, and another rooster was welded to protrude from the center of each hubcap. The more roosters and horses, Conte guessed, the higher your macho rating among your fellow jeepneymen.

The windshield was almost completely obscured by hood mirrors and metal animals, and, as if in compensation, a bank of six air horns extended out over it. Three more were mounted over the radiator, surrounded by an array of amber, red, and yellow beacons, reflectors, and six pairs of headlights. Conte imagined the lights drew enough current to light up his old neighborhood.

"Hey, Pops! I'm drivin', but I ain't jivin'."

The driver was hanging both arms out the window and leaning his chin on the sill, but when Conte looked up he hopped out and swung open the door, grabbing up Conte's bag without asking. Conte let him toss it inside. The driver was a slim-hipped Filipino who looked twenty.

"Couple-five more fares, Pops, and we are groovin'."

"Uh-uh," Conte said.

"Hey Pops, baby needs a new pair of shoes."

Conte showed him a fifty-peso note, then stuffed it into the kid's shirt pocket behind a pack of Marlboros. The door of the passenger compartment popped open. "Let's boogie, Pops," the driver suggested with great good cheer. Conte was pleasantly surprised to find that the interior was air-conditioned; in the three minutes between it and the terminal, his shirt was already plastered to his torso.

The driver's getup was as garish as the jeepney's exterior. His hair was carefully dressed with some substance that was thick and shiny as axle grease, combed up in a tuck-and-roll in front and swept back in long arced fenders on either side; it was the kind of hairdo known during Conte's growing-up years in New York as a D.A., for "duck's ass." He wore tire-tread sandals, a green-and-gold bowling shirt with "Manny" stitched in cursive script above the breast pocket, and tight blue jeans with a fancy-looking label on the right cheek of his ass. As he climbed into the front seat, Conte got a look at the label and couldn't suppress a laugh. It read "Designer."

Conte leaned forward in the seat and said, "Hey, Manny."

"What's that Manny jive, Dad?" The driver spoke in a lilting singsong, though his English was not particularly accented. "Oh, you mean the shirt? Hey, I did you, Cat. I'm hep to what you're puttin' down." He dug out the cigarette pack, shook one loose, and inexplicably stuck it behind his ear. Immediately the paper began to discolor as it soaked up hair grease.

"You know where Moriones Street in Tondo is?" Conte asked.

The driver did something under the dash, and stereo music hit the jeepney like a thunderclap: Mitch Ryder and the Detroit Wheels, doing "Devil with a Blue Dress On."

"I ain't no bowlster, Man," the driver shouted over the music. "I just—dig it, Dad—I just *found the shirt*." For some reason this sent him into paroxysms of insane laughter.

"Elvis, Pops," the driver got out when he was able to begin to control himself. "Elvis is the sign, and I ain't lyin'."

"Hey, Elvis," Conte hollered. "You know where Moriones Street in Tondo is?"

The jeepney swung left, past a hospital; ahead Conte could see the harbor. They turned right on the last street, a broad four-laner divided by a parkway, according to a street sign "M. Roxas Boulevard." The modern high-rise office buildings of downtown Manila loomed about a mile ahead. Elvis the driver fiddled with the sound system again, and Mitch Ryder was cut off in mid-yowl to be replaced by Jerry Lee Lewis doing "Great Balls of Fire" at—Conte would not have believed it possible—an even higher decibel level.

"I saw him once," the driver sang out suddenly, and Conte, despite himself, said, "Who?"

"Jerry Lee—get hep, Dad, get hep. Saw him right at the airport, almost got in my jeepney—hey, Man, I'm jivin', I got to tell. Saw a cat who looked like him once. That's the Matthew, Mark, Luke, and John, Pops."

They were on A. Bonifacio Boulevard now and the jeepney shot through a park that bordered the street on either side. Conte caught glimpses of people strolling among palm, banyan, and acacia; in one place there was a stand of bamboo. A couple of blocks inland toward the city center were the tourist districts of Ermita and Intramuros, the skyline dotted with familiar signs like Holiday Inn, Hilton, and Hyatt Regency.

"But Elvis, Hepcat, he was the King," the other Elvis was chattering. "Ain't no one can sing like the King, and that's the skinny—not now, not ever. Won't never be another King." Through the heart-thumping music Conte heard a note of wistfulness. "You know the King, Man?"

"Not personally."

"Sure you do," the driver said, like he had heard nothing. "Everyone knows the King."

The park dropped away and they were crossing the Pasig River. On the other side the city changed radically and immediately; Conte doubted this was part of the normal tourist's grand promenade. The San Nicolas district was part slum, part industrial zone; the jeepney slewed around a gentle half-curve to the right, and on either side of the M. Roxas Boulevard Extension, Conte could see squat, gray cement-block factory buildings with long rows of blue-tinted windows, trailer-truck depots, and Quonset hut warehouses. The jeepney jolted over railroad tracks that fanned out into siding serving the piers of the North Harbor, and the industrial area finally gave in to the slums.

Conte saw iron-roofed tenements that had to be hot as blast furnaces on days like this. Clothing, ripening fruit, and people of various sizes and colors hung from the windows. The buildings seemed designed and placed with no planning nor regard for aesthetics or sense, jumbles of tin and wood and hollow concrete blocks stacked almost one atop another. Whenever the tenements left a spare patch of ground, someone had thrown up a bamboo and nipa-thatch hut or lean-to, and each seemed to be bursting at the seams with small brown children, racing out to shout happily as the jeepney flashed past. Dogs, pigs, and goats ran in the street, and garbage seemed everywhere.

The history of rock and roll according to Elvis had progressed to the Chiffons and the Shirelles, the driver oblivious to Conte's lack of interest. Conte leaned forward in the seat.

"Hey, Elvis." Conte's mouth was inches from the driver's ear, and he shouted loud enough to hurt. "You know where Moriones Street in Tondo is?"

The driver flicked a dashboard switch, and the music went absolutely dead in the middle of a note. The silence was shattering. Elvis half-turned in his seat.

"Be cool, Man."

Conte looked in the direction he was pointing—at a street sign that read "Moriones," and below it in smaller letters, "Dist. of Tondo."

Small children were clambering onto the fenders of the idling vehicle. The air smelled of garbage. "*This* is Tondo?" Conte said incredulously.

"No, Pops, it's the Grand Ole Opry," the driver said.

Conte fished a slip of paper out of his shirt pocket. "You know where this is?"

"I'm hep, Dad." Elvis ground the jeepney back into gear. "We're flyin', 'cause I ain't lyin'."

They went down Moriones toward the piers, cutting left about twenty yards inland from the railroad spur into an alley hardly wider than Elvis's rig. Three chickens clucked their outrage and flapped into the air; it looked like one of them was clipped by the air horns, although Conte could not be sure. The jeepney squealed to a stop just before the alley ran out.

This house was of adobe, faded and cracked in places, but showing signs of being in decent repair. It had a tile roof, barred windows, and a thick wooden door with a latch handle big as a baseball bat.

"Do your thing, Pops," Elvis said. "I'm late but I'll wait."

"What do I owe you?"

Elvis's gaze narrowed. "No jive, Pops," he said in as serious a tone as he was able to muster. "This ain't no place to take your case—not alone. It ain't where it's at for your kind of cat. It ain't the hive for your—"

"How much, Elvis?"

" 'Nother fifty pesos, Pops," the driver said sullenly. "I ain't no money hound."

Conte dropped a one hundred-peso note in the kid's lap. "Buy yourself some new dialogue."

"Thanks, Pops." Elvis revved the motor. "It's your funeral." Alley gravel sprayed against sheet-metal walls when he sped off.

Conte watched the jeepney swing back onto Moriones, while the small children watched him. He could feel the eyes on him when he knocked on the thick wooden door. He got out a cigarette, lit it, and he was raising his hand to knock again when the door fairly burst open.

The man had a brown wrinkled face, no front teeth at all, and no hair beyond a gray fringe like a monk's tonsure. Conte put his age at fifty—but that didn't mean he'd be interested in drawing the guy as a sparring partner.

The sleeveless white T-shirt he wore showed off arms that bulged with a lifetime of muscle, above a stomach flat as a butte. He stared at Conte through sharp dark eyes and hitched at his bell-bottomed trousers.

"I'm looking for—"

"Come," the man said. He had a deep, thick voice and an accent that sounded almost West Indian.

Before Conte could say anything else, the man grabbed his biceps in a vise grip and walked him into the house. The door slammed behind him.

If a lunatic asylum held a rummage sale, Conte thought, it would look like the house's front room. Junk was jumbled everywhere, nearly hiding the collection of dilapidated furniture. Newspapers, magazines, clothes, tools, and fishing gear were stacked in precarious piles. There were transistor radios, calculators, and other inexpensive electronics items, most with parts of the plastic cases missing and their wires hanging out like a samurai's intestines. An entire corner of the room was devoted to weapons, from an American M16 with the receiver assembly missing to a wicked-looking scythe.

"You like my collection, eh?" The big man walked Conte on through the room without waiting for an answer. At least it was cool in the dimly lit house, well below the ninety-five degrees toward which the day was climbing.

The kitchen was uncluttered only by comparison. Pots, pans, dishes, and utensils were arranged without particular concession to logic, but there was a cleared space in the center in which a folding card table and four folding chairs presided. A female figure was bent over the sink, but before Conte could make her out further the burly middle-aged man pointed to one of the folding chairs and barked, "Sit."

"My name is—"

"SIT!" the man roared.

Conte sat.

The man lowered himself into the chair opposite. "First we eat, then we talk. Always a man must eat before talk."

"Please don't pay any attention to my father," the woman said behind Conte. Then she was leaning over his shoulder to set a covered tureen in the middle of the table. She was around thirty, perhaps a few years younger than Conte, dark with shiny, straight black hair and full sensual lips. She wore American blue jeans and a USC T-shirt; one of her breasts brushed Conte's shoulder as she turned back to the sink. "He loves to growl and order people around, until they learn the trick."

The big brown man was scowling at Conte, but Conte decided to take the chance anyway. "What's the trick?"

The young woman set another covered dish on the table. "Ignore him," she said.

The man's scowl deepened, but he waved offhandedly toward the young woman and said, "This is my fresh American-mouthed daughter, Cilla. Say hello, Conte."

Conte stared at the man. "You're Ferdinand?"

"No," the man said heavily. "I am Her Honor the Mayor Imelda Marcos's pimp." He slammed a fist into the table. "Why should I not be Ferdinand?" he demanded.

"*Padre,*" Cilla said, softly and automatically, like a mother clucking to a crying baby.

"No reason I can see," Conte said quickly.

"Good," the man snapped. He reached for the covered tureen and said again, "Eat."

Conte regarded him. Ferdinand—the Ferdinand with whom Conte was supposed to make contact—was another member of George Petrie's far-flung network. He was a free lance, an odd-job man who came recommended as a good partner in a tight spot. His usual livelihood was running a commercial fishing boat out of the North Harbor, but he was supposed to have sailed all through the thousands of miles of sea that connected the thousands of Philippine Islands. In short, he had been billed as exactly the local hand Conte would need.

But Conte had expected a younger man. In the world he' had only lately left—the world of organized crime—by the time a man was fifty he was wearing $700 suits and sitting behind a desk in a midtown office—or he didn't make it to fifty in the first place.

Cilla placed three more dishes on the table and slid into the chair to Conte's left. Her father glared at her and began to ladle from the tureen into a bowl, which he passed to Conte.

"I hope you like everything," Cilla said to him. She spoke perfect unaccented English. "You can see how great a store my father places by food, so I'm supposed to have become a fine cook." She pointed to the bowl into which Conte was staring with some trepidation. "That's called *sinigang;* it's a sour soup with pork and vegetables. Those spring rolls aren't much different from what you get in an Oriental restaurant back home, except the filling includes heart of coconut; we call them *lumpia*. The *bihon*—I'm sorry, rice noodles—are good with the fish sauce, and I do hope you try some of *atchara*. That's pickled vegetables.''

Conte took a gingerly taste of the *sinigang*. It was hot and spicy and had a rich meaty flavor. He smiled and nodded politely to Cilla, and dug in.

"You went to school in the U.S.?" Conte asked.

"Yes."

"And . . ."

Cilla smiled at him. "And why am I back here, living like this? Is that what you wish to know?"

Conte reached for the *bihon*, to be doing something with his hands. "Sorry," he muttered.

"Don't be. It's a reasonable question." She paused, as if considering the right phrasing. "You see, while I was in California—"

"Eat," Ferdinand growled.

Cilla cut herself off abruptly. Okay, Conte thought, so the guy doesn't like conversation at the table. But he noticed that now Cilla was concentrating hard on the food on her plate.

No one spoke again until the meal was over and Cilla had risen and begun to clear bowls and plates. "You may smoke, Conte," Ferdinand announced in his deep voice. Conte got out the pack of Camels and was about to shake one loose when instinct gave him a better idea. He offered the pack to Ferdinand.

The other man beamed—the first time he had smiled, Conte realized. Ferdinand took the pack, solemnly extracted a single cigarette, tamped it ceremonially on the card table, and stuck it in his mouth, then folded both arms in front of him. Conte flicked the Zippo, and Ferdinand inhaled with great and evident satisfaction.

"I am Ferdinand," the big man announced, as if it were the introduction to a formal address—and in a way, it was. "This is Cilla, my daughter. Her mother, my wife, is no longer alive, so we are together, Cilla and I. She keeps my house and watches over me."

"No one watches over you, *padre*," Cilla murmured. "You will not let them."

Ferdinand scowled at the interruption. "I have my work as well," he continued. "In this Cilla helps me, too."

Conte wondered what that meant. There was something about the young woman that made Conte think that she was as much front—perhaps in a different way—as her father. A small family-owned business, he thought wryly.

"In our country," Ferdinand said, "the civilized people speak English. Cilla and I, we also speak Spanish, the language of the first colonialists in these islands, and," he added with something like a sneer, "Filipino, which is something like Tagalog and is supposed to be the national language of our people." Ferdinand placed both of his oversized palms flat on the table in front of him. "Now, my friend Conte: what more do you wish to know?"

Conte had still not decided quite what to make of this man. Instinct—and perhaps the attractive Cilla—was predisposing him in Ferdinand's direction. But on this mission, every time he brought someone else into his circle of confidence, he increased his vulnerability. The closer he got to Vancouver, the greater the chance that Vancouver would get a scent of him. If the international assassin was holed up in these islands, it stood to reason that he had a defense perimeter of some kind. And if Conte ran up against it unwittingly, he'd be a dead man before he even knew of his mistake.

"George Petrie," Conte said.

"Yes, yes," Ferdinand said impatiently, waving his cigarette in the air. "I know you are from my friend George. You would not be sitting at my table if I did not know that immediately. I ask you once more: what do you wish to know?"

"You have a boat?"

Ferdinand threw both hands over his head, like a referee signaling a touchdown. "No, friend Conte, I do my fishing from the pier, with a cork and a length of string." He laughed; it sounded something like a guard-dog's gnar. "Of course I have a boat, the finest boat in all of Tondo." Ferdinand stood up, so suddenly his folding chair nearly fell over backward. "Come."

Cilla wiped her hands on a dish towel and followed them out the back door. A narrow, garbage-filled canal ran past, separated from the rear of the house by a path no wider than three feet. The canal passed under a low railroad trestle and ran into the harbor, a hundred yards distant.

As soon as they stepped out the door there was a chorus of shouts and squeals. Conte spun on his heel, his right hand automatically reached under his left arm for the .45 automatic. But the hoard descending on the three of them were all children, brown and white and yellow, and a few with the same Hispanic-Oriental features as the brutal giant Rook, none taller than Conte's waist. In a moment they were caught up in the swarm, the children shouting, "Ferdinand, Ferdinand," with evident glee.

Ferdinand cocked both elbows like a rooster and gave a bellowing roar, deep as a diesel. Conte was surprised that so much sound could come from any one man, even one the size of Ferdinand. "Beware the claws of the great lion Ferdinand," the big brown man bellowed, and lunged at the nearest little girl.

Instead of jumping back in fright, the little girl hugged him and kissed his cheek.

"Ugh!" Ferdinand barked. He made a big show of

wiping off the kiss. "Go away, you little bandits," he ordered.

None of the children moved.

Ferdinand reached in the back pocket of his bell-bottoms and came out with a handful of something shiny. Conte looked closer; with some surprise he saw it was Hershey's Chocolate Kisses. Ferdinand threw the handful of foil-wrapped candy down the path, and the knot of children scrambled after them.

Ferdinand dusted his hands together ostentatiously. "The little beggars," he said to Conte. "It is the only way to get rid of them."

"You are an old phony, *padre*," Cilla said. To Conte she added, "He loves them as if they were his own."

Ferdinand glared at her. "What are you doing here? This is men's business."

"Then let us *men* see to it," Cilla said impudently, and led the way down the path.

The pier at which they stopped was at the far northern end of the north bay, perhaps a half mile all told from Ferdinand's house. Except for the boats moored at it, it looked like any other commercial fisherman's dock around the world. Nets hung over posts to dry, a permanent sheen of oil floated on the stagnant breakwater surface, and the smell of the catch was so thickly enmeshed with the air that you could taste it. At the shore end there was a bamboo-thatch hut with an open counter through which Conte could see engine parts, cans of motor oil, a fuel pump, and a few tools. The proprietor sat behind the counter reading a *Batman* comic book; his hands were knobby and gnarled, the fingers so badly twisted and distorted it was an effort to turn the pages.

"Hello, Bagno," Ferdinand shouted. "Does anyone ask for me, you arthritic old whoremonger?"

Bagno carefully laid his comic spine-up on the counter. "Why yes, my friend. A woman with three idiot children, every one of them as ugly as you. A matter of their support, I believe she said. I told her you would be here directly."

But then the crippled dock master looked quickly around and beckoned them closer with a nod. "There was someone, my friend. A Moro. He did not ask for you, but he was looking around your boat."

Ferdinand frowned at Conte. "Were you followed?"

"I don't know. It's possible. I don't know Manila so well that I'd definitely recognize a tail."

"Why would someone tail Conte, *padre?*"

Ferdinand was still looking at him. "I don't know, daughter. Maybe soon Conte will tell us that."

The older man was right, and Conte felt a little embarrassed. He was already in thicker with the guy than he'd planned—originally he expected to simply hire a boat, not take on a family—and it was time to either trust Ferdinand fully or get the hell out of here.

"Come," Ferdinand said. "Let us see if *The San Francisco Bay* will suit Conte's special needs."

A few of the boats nosed up to the pier were standard outboards, but most were like Ferdinand's rig. *The San Francisco Bay* was moored at the far end of the dock. It was a single outrigger, about thirty feet long with a beam of about ten. The wooden hull was dinged up everywhere Conte looked, but the paint was fresh and the exterior clean, and it appeared solid enough. Conte figured he'd have to trust Ferdinand this far anyway; he had not picked up one hell of a lot of small-boat experience living in Manhattan.

"Come aboard," Ferdinand invited.

Conte followed him down to the built-up deck that spanned the middle of the boat, supporting a single mast that was now bare of sheets or lines. The prow was pointed, but the stern was squared off, and a tiny Evinrude—it could not have been over 10 horsepower—was bracketed to it. To one side of the engine was a long-handled tiller, and under the deck was stowed the sail, ropes, tools, a jumble of engine parts, and other gear whose purpose Conte could only guess at. Everything smelled of gasoline and fish.

"Now you have seen my boat, Conte," Ferdinand said. "It is time to tell your tale."

Conte glanced at Cilla.

"I have worked with my father before, Conte," she said with evident irritation. "You can speak in front of me."

"It's not that," Conte muttered. "I think we're going to be dealing with some very tough people. The more you know, the more danger you could be in."

"You're wasting time, Conte," she said coldly.

Conte glanced at Ferdinand. The big man frowned, then reluctantly nodded.

Conte offered the pack of Camels. "I'm looking for an island," he said as Ferdinand took it.

Ferdinand leaned forward to stick the tip of his smoke in the Zippo's flame, cupping his hands around it. "The name?"

"Socorro."

Ferdinand blew out smoke. "What do you want in that place?"

"You've heard of it?"

"I didn't say that."

"Come on, Ferdinand," Conte snapped. "Let's stop playing footsies and talk like men."

"You're right, Conte," Cilla put in. "But I think you should start. You've told us nothing so far, except that you have a dangerous job to do. If you want our help, we need to know more."

Conte shook his head. "I don't think so."

Cilla stood up. "Are we finished here, *padre*?" she asked coldly.

"Wait a minute," Conte said. "Don't get your back hair up. I want passage to a place called Socorro, and I don't want half of Manila to know I'm heading there. I want to be dropped on the island—wherever the hell it is—and I want a pickup exactly twelve hours later. If I don't make the meet, that's the end of it for you. I'll pay plenty, and I'll pay in advance." Conte flicked his butt over the gunwale and watched it sizzle out. "That's all of it."

For perhaps thirty seconds Ferdinand gazed at him, the cigarette stuck in the corner of his mouth and smoke spiraling up past his dark eyes. Then he stood, stepped up on the dock, and lumbered past the dock-master's shack toward the house.

Conte stared at his retreating back until he disappeared into the jungle of shacks beyond the tracks. "Well son of a bitch," he muttered finally.

"And now, Conte," Cilla said evenly, "would you like to try it again?"

"In the pictures, she looks something like me," Cilla was saying. "Prettier, I think, but dark and tall and strong, like my father. Stronger in some ways, perhaps. She was twenty-two when she was killed."

"I'm sorry," Conte murmured.

"I didn't know her," Cilla said. "I was a baby then."

From the landfill breakwater that formed the North Harbor they had an unobstructed view of Corregidor at the mouth of Manila Bay, the island to which General Douglas MacArthur promised to return when the Japanese drove the American forces from Manila Bay in early 1942. Beyond lay the South China Sea; it was early evening now, and the sun hung a few degrees above the ocean's horizon line. The breeze was offshore, cooling and untainted with the smells of the dock.

"The Hukbalahap Rebellion began during the World War," Cilla said, staring out over the water. "My mother was only a girl then. At first it was a guerrilla movement against the Japanese invaders—the name means People's Anti-Japanese Army—but its members were all poor tenant farmers from the interior of Luzon, and when the War was over the movement continued as a people's protest against the rich landowners. Many of the wealthy had collaborated with the Japanese in exchange for protection and patronage, but even if they had not, the peasants were fed up with caciquism. Under the system, fewer than two dozen people held ninety percent of the interior land."

The leading edge of the sun touched the water, and at that moment a high-masted boat crossed its face. "My mother fought alongside the men from the time she was fourteen. Two years after that she met Ferdinand, who led another guerrilla band. They were married immediately because there was no time for courtship."

She looked at Conte. "I try to imagine their life together, but I can't. All I know is that they knew nothing but violence and fighting and pain."

"And love," Conte said.

"I hope so." Cilla shook her head. "By 1950 the Huk army was disciplined and well-organized, and they had advanced to within ten miles of Manila. Even today some people think they could have taken the city."

"What happened?"

"Someone—it had to be a member of the Council of Generals—someone betrayed them. The commanders were captured and jailed in a series of simultaneous raids, as were many of the soldiers. Ferdinand escaped, but my mother was put in a prison camp. Before Ferdinand could do anything to free her, she was dead."

"How?"

"They said she was shot trying to escape. That may be; if it isn't, we'll never know the truth. She was a lovely woman."

"So are you, Cilla."

The young woman shook her head impatiently, as if denying the compliment. "You have to understand: after it was over—the Huks were broken and my mother dead—my father became bitter, cynical. Some of it passed with time, but some of it remains. He has no use for politics or movements or rhetoric. He lives in a slum, and he accepts that. He fishes and he works for people—people like you, Conte—and he does not worry about whys or consequences. That's part of the answer to your question, why I came back to him after college in your country. I'm here because he needs me. I'm afraid that he doesn't care anymore, and at the same time I'm afraid he'll get in too deeply."

"You work with him?"

"I insist on it." She managed a wan smile. "It's the only way to keep an eye on it. He hated the idea at first, of course. But I reminded him that he fought beside my mother, and I worked on him, and finally there was nothing he could do because he saw I was right."

She startled him by placing her hand on his arm. "My father is Filipino, Conte—more than me in some ways because he's spent all his life here, and he fought for what he believed in, before he became embittered. There's a term in Tagalog—*utang na loob*. It's a way of behaving, what you could call a code of honor; it's concerned with doing the right thing, with obligations, debts."

"I can understand that." Conte was thinking of Dennison; he wondered if the boss had ever met Ferdinand.

"That's why my father was offended by you," Cilla went on. "According to *utang na loob,* because he accepted you fully—into his house, his boat, into his life—you are obligated to reciprocate. He will not serve you, but it is his honor to serve with you. Nor does he question your cause, not if you come from George Petrie, for whom we have worked before. But *hiya*—that is the Tagalog word for a sense of propriety and of shame—his *hiya* requires that you accept him as an equal."

"All that will do is put him in danger."

"My father has been in danger all his life, ever since he was a Huk. You can't change that one way or the other."

"Dammit," Conte persisted. "This is a one-man job."

Cilla pulled her hand away and turned her back to the bay. "Then do it by yourself."

"I'm only trying to protect—"

"Protect yourself, Conte. My father and I can take care of ourselves."

The sun was a half circle sitting on the water now, crowned by a halo of brilliant red and yellow. Conte sighed. "This isn't the first time you've been involved with something like this, is it?" When she said nothing, he went on. "What kind of work . . . ?"

"The dangerous kind, Conte. You don't have to worry about us covering your back."

Conte shook his head. There was too much at stake here to make a mistake—but dammit, there were already enough lives at risk. Melinda Bannister could already be dead, and hell, there was his own skin to worry about as well. From what he knew of Vancouver, he'd be a fool to underestimate the danger he represented.

Besides that, he still hadn't shaken the habit of

working alone, even after the operation against Frank Bressio in the Nevada desert when he had teamed with Bill Price, Vang, and Chris Amado. Funny, he thought suddenly: Chris and Cilla had a lot in common, from spirit to looks. Maybe that was something to keep in mind. . . .

"Listen," Conte said. He put a hand on her shoulder.

He felt her stiffen, but finally she turned and looked at him. "What is it?"

Conte gave her a faint smile. "Let's go find Ferdinand," he said. "It looks like I've got a story you and he ought to hear."

Chapter Seven

Everything about the mission so far had set Conte on edge; he felt like the only actor in a play who hadn't been given a script.

The bar did nothing to calm his nerves.

It was a dark smoky place in the half basement of an anonymous brick loft building, identifiable only by a partially burned-out electric sign reading "L Q OR." This was the Pandacan district, southeast of the city center back in the direction of the airport, a couple of hundred acres of factories and warehouses, and narrow alleys and few streetlights. It was a little after eleven at night, and the place was crowded with workers coming off the second shift, as well as a few knocking back a last drink to ease the ordeal of walking in late.

The bar was fashioned of unfinished narra wood, its reddish tinge faint in the dim light, and the shelf behind it was undecorated except for neon depictions of the logos of a half-dozen American, Filipino, and Japanese beers. The tables were beat up and set too close together, and as near as Conte could make out, the way they had come in was the only access. It would not be a pleasant place to get caught in a fire.

Actually, it was not a particularly pleasant place under any circumstances.

Ferdinand forced a path through the crowd of men— Conte saw no women—mostly through his bulk and generous use of his elbows. A tiny round table, no more than a foot across, was squeezed into one corner, and they wedged themselves into the chairs, their backs to the wall.

The customers were uniformly dark skinned, with Malaysian features; many wore turbans and skintight cotton trousers. Conte caught several of them shooting him and Ferdinand the same kind of looks Conte would expect to get if he crashed a rent party on Amsterdam Avenue. Men spoke with heads close together, darting looks at their corner table, and the pitch of the buzz of conversation subtly changed. The gist of it was evident: as far as the patrons were concerned, he and Ferdinand were definitely not welcome here.

Conte had the uncomfortable feeling they were about to try to do something about it.

That afternoon, in the cluttered kitchen of the Tondo house, Ferdinand had briefed him on the Moros. They were Muslims, and a minority; 85 percent of Filipinos were Roman Catholic, the religion imported from Spain in the 1500s by Magellan and the clergy that followed on his heels. Ironically, Islam had arrived two centuries earlier, introduced—sometimes by force—by the Arab traders and Indonesian missionaries who visited the Philippines beginning in the fourteenth century.

The Moros practiced a fairly unorthodox form of the religion—for one thing, the prohibition against alcohol was pretty much ignored, as Conte could see. But they were totally committed to its defense. To the Moros, Islam stood for the way of life before the Spanish invaders, so their allegiance to it was nationalistic as well as religious.

In the seven centuries since Islam had been introduced to the islands, the Moros had become convinced that they would always be victimized by oppression and bigotry, so they learned to fight like hellcats. For thirteen years after the turn of the century, when the rest of the islands had resigned themselves to U.S. sovereignty, the Moros, based mostly on Mindanao and the islands of the Sulu Archipelago, fiercely resisted. Guerrilla warfare and terrorism persisted to this day, Ferdinand said; since the Moro *datu*, or chief, Utdong Matalam, formed the Mindanao Independence Movement in 1968, thousands had died and as many as 1.5 million people of the southern islands had been driven from their homes.

"Now there is talk the Moros have Communist backing," Ferdinand said, sitting in his cluttered kitchen. "This Qaddafi in Libya, he has proclaimed support for all Muslims everywhere, and they say he is sending weapons and money to the Moros. In the southern islands where they fight, there is no such thing as an innocent person. Fighting for what one believes, that is all right. But killing women and burning villages is something again."

Conte nodded his agreement, but from the corner of his eye he was watching Cilla as she finished the cleaning chores at the sink. She had coached him on his apology to her father; on her advice he had pleaded good faith, ignorance of local custom, and a misplaced desire to avoid involving him in danger that was rightfully his to risk.

Ferdinand listened gravely and sat without moving for long moments after Conte finished. Finally he reached his bearlike paw across the table, and Conte took it. The man had a grip like a bench-vise. After that it was all right.

"Vancouver," Ferdinand repeated, rolling his name around on his tongue. "And a place named Socorro, eh?" He pursed his lips. "I have heard talk, vague rumors." Then he brightened. "There is a place we can go . . ."

He pounded a fist into the table, his standard method, it appeared, of attracting Cilla's attention. "You will go to the city, daughter."

"I will go with you."

Ferdinand grinned broadly, knowing he had this argument won from the start. "This place we are going— women are not allowed."

"Of course not," Cilla said skeptically. "They never are."

"I would not lie, daughter. Now then: you will go into the city and stay there until tomorrow."

"What are you talking about, *padre*?"

"There were men asking about me, as Bagno told us this afternoon. I do not like that. For now, you do as I tell you." Ferdinand stood and stretched. "It is time for a nap. There will be much to do this night."

From the front room Conte heard the crash as Ferdinand dumped the contents of the couch to the floor, and then the springs whine in protest as the big man stretched out. He waited politely, but Cilla did not seem to have anything more to say. But when he went outside to smoke, he was only half-done with the cigarette before she joined him.

"I wanted to tell you . . ." he started, but before he could get it out she was nestled up against him, and her lips were on his. Conte started to pull her closer, but she wrestled free. "Later," she breathed. "When you come back. For now, a kiss for luck."

She pushed a strand of dark hair away from her cheek. "You're at my mercy now, Conte," she said lightly. "If my father finds out you kissed me, he'll kill you."

Conte laughed lightly. "Now you're kidding me."

"Are you sure?" She stepped close once more, and her lips brushed the side of his neck. "Later," she murmured again, and then the evening swallowed her up.

*   *   *

"The south islands," Ferdinand muttered again in the dingy Moro bar.

"What did you say?" Conte said, startled out of his recollection.

"If a man wanted solitude in the Philippines," Ferdinand explained, "the south islands would be the first place to seek it." He leaned across the table and lowered his rumbling voice. "The rumors about this Socorro that I have heard: it is in the south islands that they place this magical hideaway. Somewhere in the Sulu Sea, maybe, near the west coast of Mindanao, or maybe in the archipelago where there are hundreds of tiny droppings of land. That is why we are here." He made a sweeping gesture that encompassed the room. "Nothing happens in the south islands without the Moros knowing."

But Conte's attention had shifted again. Across the crowded, dingy bar a man had come through the door leading up to the street, squinting and craning his neck to see around the joint before his gaze lit on their table. He started to make his way toward them, and had a time of it. He was dark skinned and Malaysian-looking like the other patrons, but he was no more than five six, slightly built, and almost delicate looking, a little effeminate. He tried to elbow between two beefy factory workers, and one of the men turned and put a palm in the middle of his chest and shoved him, so he jostled and nearly upset a table. A couple of beer bottles toppled, but the skinny man scuttled into the anonymity of the crowd before he could be further abused. Conte lost sight of the guy—until a few seconds later when he popped up at the side of their table.

"I am here, Ferdinand." He had a whining nasal voice, and English so thickly accented Conte could barely make out the words. "My friend, when you call, I come here without a hesitate, to partake of the company of your—"

"Sit down," Ferdinand ordered.

The man sat abruptly in the vacant chair, fussing with his tight trousers before folding both hands primly on the table.

"His name is Tamal," Ferdinand said to Conte with evident distaste, like a man introducing his ugly mother-in-law.

"We are greatest friend, Ferdinand and I," Tamal babbled in his annoying whine. "It is only of the finest of my pleasure to see you again, my greatest friend."

Ferdinand leaned forward so his face was no more than six inches from Tamal's. The skinny man's dark skin looked suddenly ashen. "Socorro," Ferdinand said in a very low voice.

Tamal opened and closed his mouth several times, like a guppy at feeding time.

"Where is it?" Ferdinand said, and added sarcastically, "Tell me, my greatest friend."

Tamal shook his head. When he managed to find his voice again, he said, "I don't know."

"You are lying, and it is a sin to lie." There was such menace in Ferdinand's voice he might have been invoking the condemnation himself. "Tell me, you miserable piece of dog shit, or I will hurt you very badly."

Tamal tried to push his chair back—and ran into another man. The man paid no attention; he was staring at Matt Conte.

"They say you are asking the wrong questions, Ferdinand." The newcomer had a big voice and a body to match, and there was a five-inch curve of scar from his left ear along his jawline to the point of his chin. "What are you doing away from Tondo and asking such, Ferdinand?"

Finally he took his gaze from Conte and turned it on the other man. "Sometimes if you ask the wrong questions, you get answers you would not like." He leaned over Tamal and said something in Tagalog, but its tone conveyed the thrust of its threat.

Tamal let out a low moan. His clasped hands were trembling.

"Get out of here," Ferdinand snapped. Tamal did not need to be told twice. He was up on shaking legs and swallowed by the crowd almost before Ferdinand finished speaking.

"Take your own advice," the man said in his hard dead voice. "No one will answer your wrong questions, so do not ask them again, here or elsewhere"—he turned his vicious gaze on Conte once more—"unless you wish such pain you will remember it for a lifetime."

The man shifted his weight slightly, and Conte saw his knuckles whiten as he pushed down on the little round tabletop. There was a splintered tearing sound as the bolts pulled free of the wood's grain, and then with a single wrenching jerk the man ripped the top from its pedestal and threw it to one side. Someone yelped with surprise or hurt. The man barked a laugh in Ferdinand's face and turned away, bulling his way into the crowd's mass.

The pitch of conversation rose, and Conte realized that for the last minute or so they had been the center of attention again. He was not inclined to protest when Ferdinand said, "We might as well go. He is Batu, the bully chief of the Moros in this district, and by now he has put out the order. So he is right: there is no man here who will speak with us. I am sorry, my friend."

"Not your fault, Ferdinand. It looks like this Batu has them nailed down."

"Still, I do not like to have the others think Batu can

order us around. For you it is maybe okay, but I must operate in this city of Manila."

Conte remembered what Cilla had said about *hiya*, the sense of self-esteem and honor. Conte appreciated Ferdinand's position, but right now *hiya* would have to take a back seat. The clock was running, and none of this was bringing him closer to Vancouver, and Melinda Bannister— not to mention the file marked "Top Secret" she was carrying in her head.

"No matter," Ferdinand said abruptly. Conte noticed something in his tone and expression that had not been there before: worry. Cilla popped into mind again. Of course: Ferdinand was thinking of what Bagno the dock master had said about snooping strangers.

"Right." Conte stood. "Let's get back." The look Ferdinand shot him was so penetrating he felt suddenly uncomfortable. "She'll be all right," he said lamely.

Ferdinand was already clearing a path toward the door, and Conte hustled into his wake. Dark faces glared hostilely from both sides, and Conte could feel the eyes on the back of his neck as the crowd melded together again behind him. He stumbled over someone's deliberately extended foot and pretended not to notice; the last thing they needed was a bar brawl in which they were outnumbered twenty-five to one.

Ferdinand was waiting outside on the broken sidewalk. "She likes you, Conte."

"What'd you say?" He was breathing a little hard.

"I do not want to see her hurt," Ferdinand said gruffly. "By anyone." His tone made it clear that "anyone" included present company.

"Let's get back," Conte said. The nearest streetlight was at the corner half a block down, but here it was nearly pitch dark. A slight breeze had come up since they had entered the bar, enough to cool the night air but not enough to cleanse from it the stink of the paint factory.

"Yes," Ferdinand said, oddly formal. "Let us get back."

Ferdinand's car was a twenty-year-old bathtub Porsche; they had parked it on Taft Avenue, a thoroughfare with plenty of traffic and at least a little more light, three and a half blocks from the nameless bar.

They had covered one of those blocks when the guy with the knife lunged out of the alley.

Conte flattened against the brick wall of the factory they were passing, as Ferdinand jumped away from the attacker, graceful as a man half his size and bulk. Instead of thrusting again, the knifeman darted back, and before Ferdinand could regain his balance, a deep voice said, "Do not move."

Conte's hand was halfway to his shoulder holster. He let it rest on his belt buckle, trying to make the move look natural.

Batu stepped out of the shadow, flanked by a man with an AK-47, the Russian submachine gun. "Shoot to kill if either of them moves," Batu ordered in his deadly voice.

Ferdinand stood motionless, his hands loose at his sides. Batu took his time approaching, a faint superior smile on his dark face. In the dimness the line of scar tissue along his jaw seemed too white.

Batu balled his fist and hit Ferdinand in the middle of the face.

Ferdinand's head bounced back against the brick of the wall, and blood sprayed from his nose. Ferdinand shook his head slightly and straightened his shoulders, then did not move. The man with the AK-47 shot a look at the action, then brought his attention back to Conte.

Conte inched his hand up to his chest.

"There is more pain for you this night, Ferdinand," Batu said. "For the questions you have already asked, and so you do not ask them again." His hand blurred in the darkness, and Ferdinand's head snapped to one side, hard enough so blood splattered audibly against brick.

The gunner's slack mouth had fallen open at the sound. He blinked at Conte, then turned his head for another quick peek at the action.

Conte jerked the Colt .45 free from leather and shot the gunner in the chest. The machine gun clattered on the pavement and the guy lived long enough to slap both hands on the hole over his heart before that muscle gave its last spasm and he went down.

Ferdinand slammed a knee up between Batu's legs, and the Moro squealed like a shoat. Instinctively he grabbed at himself and bent double. This time Ferdinand's knee caught him in the face, with the wrenching sound of bone and cartilage shattering into fragments. Batu fell to the ground and curled into a ball, one hand cupping his crushed testicles, the other clawing at his face, as if he could pluck away the pain.

The knifeman looked at Conte's gun. He took a step backward and the blade fell from his fingers, as if he had forgotten he was supposed to hold on to it.

Conte extended the gun toward him, and the man spun away and scrambled off into the darkness.

Ferdinand was down on one knee, crouching over Batu's writhing form. Blood dripped from Ferdinand's chin.

"Are you all right?" Conte said huskily.

Instead of answering, Ferdinand grabbed two fistfuls of Batu's loose shirt. He pulled the Moro upright without apparent effort, propping him against the wall. Batu's eyes rolled open.

"Where is Socorro?" Ferdinand said.

Batu snapped something pithy in Tagalog.

Without taking his eyes from the Moro, Ferdinand said to Conte, "Kill him."

Conte moved closer, and Batu's eyes opened wider. Conte let him see the big bore of the .45 automatic.

He bent and lay the warm muzzle against the space between the Moro's bushy eyebrows. He pushed hard, twisting the barrel against the flesh, deliberately trying to hurt the man.

"I am dead," Batu said, in a curiously detached tone. What had been his nose was now a shapeless blob of flesh mashed up against his cheek, next to a ragged rip in his skin. Blood pulsed weakly from the tear.

"That's right," Conte snapped. "Now answer the man."

"Socorro," Ferdinand hissed.

"Let's finish this up," Conte said softly. "That gunshot is going to bring company, sooner or later."

"Oh, no," Ferdinand said smoothly, staring into Batu's dark dead eyes. "These Moros, they are always shooting people up—others, themselves—it doesn't matter. When Marcos declared martial law and told everyone to turn in their unregistered guns, these Moros told him to go to hell, so in the end he had to make a special rule for them. These Moros, they like blood and pain."

Ferdinand hawked and spit, catching Batu in the chin. Spittle mixed with blood and ran down his dark neck.

"Kill the bastard," Ferdinand said.

Conte cocked the .45 and jabbed the barrel into the gory gap where Batu's nose had been—and was rewarded by a whimper of agony.

"What?" Ferdinand said sharply.

"Your word," Batu moaned. "If I tell you I live."

"If you tell, we won't kill you," Conte corrected. The key to interrogation was fear, and once the man showed the first flash of it, Conte wanted to keep it rolling.

"Talk," Ferdinand ordered.

Batu seemed to sigh, and when he spoke his voice was mechanical, detached, the rhythms of his Tagalog staccato, unaccented.

In the distance Conte heard the first faint sounds of a siren.

"If you have told a lie," Ferdinand said,. "I will come for you. Remember that, you son of a whore."

"I swear—" Batu began.

Ferdinand grabbed his ears and slammed his head back against the brick wall, and Batu's neck went limp. The sirens were getting closer.

Ferdinand rose with something approaching leisure. The bleeding from his nose was mostly stopped, although his shirt was stiff with blood, black-red in the darkness. Three blocks down toward Taft, tires squealed on pavement and flashing red lights hove into view.

"We had better get some rest, my friend," Ferdinand said, his dignity unruffled by the approaching police cars. "We ship for Socorro tomorrow, and it is always best to be under sail before dawn."

He disappeared into the alley that had hidden the knifeman, and Conte darted after him.

Chapter Eight

If he had not been lying fully awake, she might have died: afterward Conte kept telling himself that, but it didn't make him feel much better.

It had been well after midnight when he and Ferdinand returned, but Cilla was awake, sitting in the jumbled living room and reading. When she saw the blood covering the front of her father's shirt her eyes widened, but she asked no questions until she had fetched soap, water, and antiseptic and tended to his face. Even then she said only, "Did you learn what you wished to?" When her father nodded, she smiled. "After I see to you, I will get ready." Ferdinand scowled but did not bother to tell her she was not coming along, either putting it off until he felt stronger or giving it up as useless.

After the blood was wiped away, the wound did not look as serious; his nose was swollen and probably fractured, but Ferdinand's breathing was normal, and there would be no long-term damage beyond the cosmetic.

"It will make me all the more handsome," Ferdinand joked. "It will add to the fine character of my face."

"If your face gets any more character, *padre*," Cilla replied, "you will be so ugly you will frighten yourself when you look in the mirror."

But tension underlay the bantering. The were committed now, and all three of them knew it. Word of the scene in the bar—not to mention the dead man in the alley—would surely get back to Vancouver, if the loyalty of Batu and his thugs was any indication. That meant that aside from the threat posed by Melinda Bannister, Vancouver had to be stopped—or Conte, Ferdinand, and Cilla would all be looking over their shoulders for the rest of their lives.

Which might not be that long.

Cilla was the one who put it into words. Ferdinand had gone to sleep immediately after she had finished patching him up; he simply flopped back on the swaybacked sofa and began to snore. Conte went out the back and stood over the canal, finishing a final smoke.

"Finding this man Vancouver is very important to you, isn't it?" Cilla was suddenly at his elbow.

"To you, too," Conte said softly.

"What has he done?"

"It doesn't really matter," Conte said. "He stole something that he has no right to, and if I don't get it back all of us will be in deep shit." Conte smiled humorlessly into the darkness. All this was still new to him. A couple of months earlier, his only concern had been a $50,000 price on his corpse, and too many men with too many guns out to collect it. But that was before Dennison caught up with him—

And sent him out to save the world.

Cilla nestled up against him and put her arm around his waist, and they stood that way until he took the last drag of his cigarette and flicked the butt into the middle of the canal, hearing the hiss and seeing the tiny light of its ember blink out. When she kissed him it was almost chaste, her lips barely brushing his before she pulled him close and held him for a long time.

"It matters," she murmured, as if she had heard his thoughts. "Always remember it does, Conte."

He was lying on his back an hour later, hands folded

beneath his head and eyes staring up at nothing, turning over her words in his mind, when he heard her scream.

Conte sat bolt upright and grabbed for the .45 on the floor beside him before scrambling up from the mattress Cilla had laid out for him in the kitchen. The night was still warm, and he wore only boxer shorts.

Cilla started to scream again, and then the sound abruptly cut off, like a phonograph record when someone lifts off the needle.

Her bedroom was off the front room, and the door was ajar. Conte raised the .45 in both hands and charged through it.

He was too late to save Cilla, but he was in time to see a man die.

At the moment he came through the door, everyone was still as a painting. He pulled himself up so short he almost lost his balance.

The big bulk of Batu was backed into the corner to Conte's left, his shoulders warily hunched, his hands away from his side ready for movement. There was a wad of gauze where his nose should have been. Ferdinand faced him, blocking escape.

Cilla lay on her back atop the mattress in the opposite corner. The covers had been torn away, and she was nude, her arms outstretched, her fine legs slightly splayed.

The haft of a knife stuck out of her lower abdomen, and blood wormed down from the embedded blade to puddle among the bedclothes.

Batu snorted and pulled another like it from his waistband. He shifted his weight to the balls of his feet, ready to thrust.

Ferdinand bellowed a raging animal cry and closed on the Moro.

Batu slashed at Ferdinand's face, and Ferdinand slapped the knife out of Batu's hand without looking at it, as if he were shooing away an insect. The knife flew across the room and landed at Conte's feet.

Batu's face was drawn and pale as he stared at Ferdinand. Conte could not see Ferdinand's expression, but he knew what it looked like.

It looked like death.

Batu saw the same thing, and he feinted left and then tried to slip past on the right, but Ferdinand's hands shot out quick as thought, fingers crabbed to lock around Batu's thick throat. Batu's eyes bulged in their sockets, and his tongue oozed from his mouth like toothpaste from a tube. He tried to claw at Ferdinand's eyes and could not reach them, and then he tried grabbing at the fingers vise-locked around his windpipe but they would not work right, and his eyeballs looked big as grapes.

Ferdinand grunted softly, and there was a louder, sharper sound, as if someone had stepped on a dry twig, and Batu's neck bone snapped cleanly as a pretzel stick. His bug-eyes shrank and went opaque, and blood bubbled from the corner of his mouth.

Ferdinand shook the limp body once, like a dog might shake a rubber toy, then tossed it aside like a beanbag.

Conte blinked hard, almost as if he expected all of this to disappear when he opened his eyes. Then he was down beside Cilla's sprawled body.

Her soft breasts were rising and falling weakly.

"She's alive," he said over his shoulder.

Ferdinand pushed him aside so roughly he toppled from his crouch onto his hands and knees.

"Leave the knife where it is," Conte rasped. "Pulling it might only hurt her worse."

Ferdinand made no sign that he heard, but he left the

knife alone. He slid his massive arms under his daughter's shoulders and knees and lifted her from the bed, gentle as a newborn.

Conte yanked a blanket from the tangle on the mattress, and blood splashed from it.

When he draped it over her, his eyes met Ferdinand's.

The big man's gaze was hard and cold and piercing, the accusation within it evident. Conte grasped for a response, but there was no response with any kind of meaning, and finally he had to look away, feeling impotent and responsible and somehow vaguely soiled.

Chapter Nine

He was thirty-four years old but he looked younger, partly because his blond hair was as thick and full as it had been twenty years earlier, partly because his open, classically Aryan features were absolutely unlined, partly because he was slim waisted and long limbed and moved with the sort of languid insouciant grace that one might associate with a slightly rebellious teenager. He wore khaki twill slacks, a plain white T-shirt that was loose enough not to bind during quick movement, and blue Nike tennis shoes. Around him as he descended the slope of the molave forest were the sounds of monkeys' frenetic chatter, the rustling leaves of the ipil and kamagong trees, the thrush of birds overhead, but he made no sound. To someone observing from a distance, he would appear to be gliding a few inches above the ground, his feet making no contact with anything solid.

In fact several people were watching, though they knew from experience his feet were securely anchored to earth.

His name was not Vancouver, but that was how he was called, and that was the name by which he thought of himself, when he thought of himself at all. His former name—the other person he had been once—had neither application nor relevance anymore. He had left that name behind, had left other parts of himself as well, in another time, in another country.

Ahead, the slope leveled into flat lowland, and beyond

it he could hear the faint crash of the surf. The molave forest gave out and yielded to the *cogonales*. He paused for a moment on the edge, then moved out into the tall coarse cogon grass. It grew about to his chin, not quite high enough to conceal him completely.

But it served the others quite well.

He looked out over the grass, turning slowly through all 360 degrees of a circle. He inhaled deeply several times, his nostrils flaring, and twice he rose up on his toes.

From the pocket of his slacks he removed a black silk handkerchief, folded neatly in quarters. He shook it out, then holding it by opposite corners, twirled it into a sash, which he banded across his eyes and knotted at the back of his head.

When he moved out into the *cogonales* again, it was with the same smooth soundless step he had used while sighted.

He was two-thirds of the way to the beach when they came at him.

At first glance they might have been triplets. Each stood about four and a half feet tall and had dark brown skin tinged with yellow, tight black hair kinky as lamb's wool, and a low-browed, big-nosed, flat face. Barefoot, naked except for tapa-cloth slings that cupped their genitals, they looked like something from prehistory. One of them carried a curved scythe, another a machete with a blade a foot long. The third had a Lüger automatic pistol, because Vancouver had left one to be stolen. They came silently, and all at once.

The one with the Lüger pulled up and fired at a range of five yards, holding the 9 mm gun with both hands against the muzzle climb, but Vancouver was somewhere else already and the slug whined harmlessly by his ear. He let his momentum carry him forward in a low dive, the scythe whistling over him a split second before the crown of his head hit the little black man wielding it two inches beneath his bare navel. At the same instant Vancouver brought both arms around in a scissors blow, the edges of his palms inward, shattering the Pygmy's rib cage and driving shards of bone through a variety of vital organs.

Vancouver's hands hit ground and pressed and he flipped heels over head, slicing through the cogon grass. The one with the Lüger was able to fire twice more before Vancouver launched himself again, this time feet first. The soft rubber soles of the Nikes hit the gunman in the forehead and he went down on his back and did not move; his skull was fractured as neatly as a coconut tapped on a sharp rock.

The one with the machete wailed with panic and crashed away through the tall grass.

Vancouver bent and his right hand closed unerringly over the haft of the scythe. He raised it over his head like an antenna, the long curved blade glistening in the tropical sunlight, and stood like that for several seconds, absolutely motionless.

Then his arm swung around in a lazy circle and the scythe went flying over the grass, whirling like a boomerang.

Except it did not come back. There was a dull thumping sound, and then silence came over the *cogonales* again.

Vancouver reached behind his head and unknotted the blindfold. He shook it out, refolded it in quarters, and replaced it in the back pocket of his twill slacks.

The first two lay on their backs on either side of him, dark eyes open and staring into the sun, their corpses free of visible blemish. Vancouver found the third of the small black men twenty-five yards toward the beach. This one lay on his stomach. On one side of his torso was the glistening scythe, and on the other his severed head.

Vancouver turned his back on the mess and returned toward the forest.

The village was in a clearing halfway up the slope, and he stopped there long enough to tell the headman where to find the bodies. The headman was old and stooped, so he looked shorter than the others, and his skin, like his hair, seemed to have gone from black to gray with age. He listened and nodded and said nothing. Women and children came out of their huts to watch him walk on, and young men stepped out of his path and were careful to keep their eyes down.

A few hundred yards further on he came into the clearing. The house stood on teakwood stilts, with open thatched walls and a thatched roof, but there were electrical wires running to an outbuilding, and the hum of a diesel generator was faintly audible. Four steps led up to the canopied porch.

The big Chinese-Filipino *mestizo* Rook came down then and stood waiting. He wore khaki shorts and nothing else. There was a three-inch ridge of scar tissue on one cheek, and the little finger of his right hand was taped to the ring finger. But he had healed rapidly; the only sign of his bullet wound was a small puckered scar on his upper arm.

"There is a report," Rook said. "Men asking questions." Vancouver listened to the rest of it with no change of expression, without even a nod of comprehension. When Rook finished, Vancouver said, "The woman?"

Rook nodded over his shoulder.

This clearing was the highest point on the island, and a light breeze always blew through the open sidewalls of the house. Inside, it was dim and cool, and the air held a vague fragrance. Vancouver went through a sitting room, down a

short corridor, and paused for a moment before a closed
door, fastened with a combination padlock. Vancouver spun
the dial, right, then left, then right once more.

Melinda Bannister wore a silk robe, brilliantly white
except for six Chinese ideograms over her left breast. She
lay on a double bed made up only with sheets, fashioned of
the same white silk; she was curled on her side, her head
propped in her cupped hand, reading a leather-bound book.

When the door opened, the book dropped out of her
hand. She sat up, scuttled on her hands back toward the
headboard, her eyes never leaving Vancouver.

The youthful-looking blond man shut the door and
came to stand at the foot of the bed. The crease in his khaki
twill slacks was sharp as a knife edge, and his white T-shirt
was spotless; there was not even any dampness under his
arms.

The front of Melinda Bannister's robe had parted,
enough to show the swell of her full breasts and the valley
between them, enough to reveal one long leg to the top of
the thigh. Her hand moved toward the hem of the robe as if
to adjust it, and then stopped.

Vancouver came around the side of the bed and stood
directly over her. He had eyes the color of polished
turquoise, and his mouth was a straight line.

Melinda Bannister's hand resumed its movement, until
it rested on the knot of the robe's sash.

Vancouver's eyes followed the movement. His head
moved, a nod that spanned perhaps a quarter of an inch.

Melinda Bannister's hand did something to the knot,
and the white silk robe fell away. She was naked underneath, her large breasts falling away slightly to either side,
the nipples standing hard and erect. The hair between her
thighs was the color of her pale blond mane, but fine and
thin, so that she seemed more naked, more exposed.

Her hand snaked lower, and her forefinger and middle finger parted the blond down and the lips they fringed.

And when he eased atop her and pressed his leg hard between hers, and his chest crushed her breasts and his mouth covered her mouth, no fear nor pain but only passion powered the fevered whimper that passed her lips.

Chapter Ten

"Here," Ferdinand said, gesturing with his knife. "Eat."

Matt Conte peered doubtfully at the offering. It looked like a strip of leather, one inch by six, that had been left out in the sun to dry and shrivel. "What is it?"

"Food," Ferdinand roared. "It is good."

Conte got a good grip on one end of the strip with his molars, but it still took both hands to tear off a bite, and a lot of jaw power to chew it. But it was good, chewy with a mild fishy flavor. "What is it?"

"Dried squid. Full of strength and power."

"How do you know?" Conte said, tearing off another mouthful.

"Ha!" Ferdinand barked. "Did you ever see a weak squid?"

Conte sat on the flat deck of *The San Francisco Bay*, Ferdinand's outrigger, his back propped against the mast. He wore jeans and no shirt, and the tropical sun was warm on his skin, though it was still morning. He'd have to watch out for sunburn; it would be foolhardy to give up any edge of stamina or mobility.

Conte gnawed off another bite of the squid and washed it down with a swig of lukewarm water from his canteen. They were in open water at last, and for at least the tenth time that morning Conte glanced over his shoulder apprehensively at the little 10 horsepower Evinrude. But the outboard continued to putt blithely along, emitting little puffs of black smoke like the Little Engine That Could.

They had left Manila an hour before dawn the previous day, and were clear of Corregidor Island and in open water by the time the leading edge of the sun cleared the hills behind Manila. They cut north of Mindoro, through the Verde Island Passage before turning due south, navigating the Tablas Strait, so they were off the west coast of the island of Antique by early evening. Conte offered to take the tiller, but Ferdinand refused to give it up. He was fine, he said; he had spent so much time on this outrigger that he could steer it in his sleep. Conte had meant to wake and check on him, but the gentle motion of the boat and the constant beat of the motor were soporific enough to put him into deep refreshing sleep for most of the night. He awoke near dawn to find Ferdinand exactly where he had been at dusk, one hand on the motor bar, scanning the sunrise horizon, and looking fresh as the new day.

"You all right?" Conte said, stretching the stiffness of sleeping on the deck from his arms and legs. He wrinkled his nose; there was a cooking smell in the air.

"I thought you would sleep the day away, Conte." Ferdinand turned and fiddled with the motor, adding over his shoulder, "Breakfast is ready." He turned back with a smoking fillet of fish on a rag, and Conte realized Ferdinand had been using the hot manifold of the motor as a grill.

"Do you fish in your sleep, too?" The fish was hot and sweet.

"Ha! I fish better in my sleep than most men with both eyes open." He was smiling broadly. "The fish know me and fight each other to get into my net. To a fish, it is an honor to be caught by Ferdinand."

But something about the big man's cheerfulness was forced, and Conte was concerned. They had raced Cilla to

San Lazaro Hospital in the Santa Cruz district, where she had been admitted in critical condition. The doctors operated immediately, and afterward she was moved to a private room which Conte had arranged and paid for in advance. He dozed on a couch in a foyer down the hall, while Ferdinand sat up beside her through the night.

The big man's callused hand on his shoulder brought Conte awake, there in the waiting room. "We must sail now," was all Ferdinand said.

Conte did not have to ask the question on his lips.

Ferdinand shrugged. "She is alive." Conte got the rest from the doctor on the way out, a brisk young Filipino named Boros: Cilla was in critical condition; her spleen, punctured in the stabbing, had been removed, and there was some sepsis. With luck and God's will—here Dr. Boros crossed himself—she would live.

Ferdinand had not mentioned his daughter since.

Neither had he given any more indication that he considered Conte in any way responsible for what had happened to the young woman. The first day at sea, hours after they cleared the harbor, he turned and said without preamble, "There in that part of Pandacan, it is the Moros who are in charge. I should have known that the police would not hold that bastard Batu for long. He had to get free to come for us because if we reached Socorro on the instructions he revealed to us, he would surely die at Vancouver's hands for his indiscretion." Conte understood this was Ferdinand's way, according to *utang na loob,* of dealing with what had happened.

But that was not what worried him. As much as Conte regretted what Batu had done to Cilla, he could not afford the liability presented by Ferdinand dwelling on it. Sure, the big man deserved his vengeance, and Conte meant to help him get it. But when the fight came down, everything you possessed—all your warrior art and personal hatred—had to be focused on the matters at hand: penetration, offense, and most of all, staying alive. Vancouver was supposed to be the most skilled killer on the planet, and they would be fighting on his home turf. If Ferdinand's mind was divided by thoughts of Cilla, that was another hairline crack in their armor for Vancouver to exploit and widen.

By now they were south of the island of Negros, perhaps 120 miles north of where Ferdinand reckoned Socorro lay. They would not reach it until after dark, Conte guessed—then the play was by the seat of the pants.

"There will be others around him," Ferdinand said suddenly. "Dangerous, and willing to fight. This is what we must guess, and prepare accordingly."

"The more people in his defensive force, the more people who know where he makes his base," Conte pointed out.

"That doesn't matter in the case of Moros." Ferdinand popped the last bit of dried squid into his mouth and chewed almost angrily. "The Moros do not give a rat's turd about Vancouver, or anyone or anything except Muslim independence. For that fight they need money, and so they are mercenaries. For example, we know that the Moros are allied with the *Partido Komunista ng Pilipinas;* in English they call themselves the New People's Army, but they are avowedly Communist, and it is an open secret that they— and through them the Moros—receive arms and money from the Russians."

"Okay, so the Moros are not the nicest guys in the world. Still, Vancouver—"

"—can offer them a great deal. He is an international outlaw, with far-flung contacts and outlets. I'm sure he pays them well and perhaps he does more, such as arranging arms deals on the international underground market, or even performing an occasional assassination for them. Remember, the Moros have always been brutal warriors in the name of Islam, and in the last ten years they have claimed responsibility for dozens of terrorist acts in which thousands have died. So if Vancouver offered the Moros aid in exchange for their services as a warning and protective network, he would be purchasing for himself a ready-made intelligence service with established branches all over the islands."

"And he could be sure the Moros would keep their mouths shut?"

"Of course. If they did not, they would lose a valuable ally, and good pay for little work—and also they would put themselves in jeopardy of Vancouver's vengeance."

Conte offered the Camels, and Ferdinand pried out the last cigarette, crumped the pack, and sent it overboard. He snatched the lighter Conte tossed to him out of the air with one hand, lit the cigarette, and threw the lighter back.

"They are almost a country unto themselves, the Moros," he said. "A country desperately desirous of freedom and willing to trample anyone along the road that leads to it." He barked out a short humorless laugh. "They are pigs," he snorted, "and a herd of them will not stop us from reaching this Vancouver. And when we do . . ." His expression darkened, and he suddenly turned away from Conte to stare out over the ocean, puffing furiously at his cigarette.

Conte followed his gaze. It was a brilliantly clear day and to the southeast he could just make out the crests of the mountains of central Mindanao; they had to be at least fifty miles distant.

Somewhere to the southwest, perhaps twice as far, lay Socorro and Vancouver and—Conte hoped upon any saints who had not already abandoned him—the missing Melinda Bannister.

Ferdinand finished his cigarette and flicked the butt out over the water, and when he looked back to Conte his quick smile had returned. "Be at ease, my friend Conte. The sea is calm and the voyage pleasant."

Ferdinand stood and stretched and turned in a slow circle, taking in the blue sameness all around them.

"Today we rest," he said evenly, "for tomorrow we fight."

Chapter Eleven

Melinda Bannister felt the length of his hardness slip from inside her, and the weight of Vancouver's body lift from hers. Her eyes had been closed, and she opened them to the whiteness of the ceiling, feeling vaguely disoriented. In her mind she had been elsewhere, with another person, but she could not remember where or with whom, only a jumble of dreamlike images, some familiar in a gauzy sort of way, some utterly alien, as Vancouver brought her to orgasm once, and then again, and then a third time as he himself soundlessly went tense and crushed hard against her before emptying himself inside.

He made love with consummate skill and no passion, and Melinda knew from experience that she would think of him for a long time, especially when she was without a man and she used her own fingers to bring herself to pleasure. Then she would screw her eyes shut and visions of his tongue and hands and cock would kaleidoscope through her mind. But in the reality of it she would quickly tire of him, because without passion a dreary sameness set in, and no matter how good it was it became mechanical, predictable, and ultimately boring.

That was the problem, she liked to tell herself: she was too easily bored.

Vancouver lay on his back beside her, his arms straight down by his sides, looking up at nothing. He looked relaxed and tense all at once, as if one part of him were constantly wound up tightly and ready for action if it was demanded. Melinda rolled over on her side, so one heavy breast rested on his chest. She traced a finger from his Adam's apple along the ridge of his breastbone, around his navel and lower, toying with the curls of his pubic hair. He had an extraordinary body, lithe and slim but with every muscle hard and defined, legs both graceful and strong enough to belong to a ballet dancer, stomach ridged with flat hard sinews. They made a handsome couple, Melinda thought sardonically.

She did not know who this man was—when she had asked his name he had replied without hesitation, but the tone in which he pronounced the three hard syllables told her not to ask any more—yet she knew he was deadly, and that she was in danger. He had killed Vince—he told her that. It was a lucky coincidence, he told her—lucky for him, not Vince. He had been in Monaco on other business, and he had recognized Andrew Vincent Dana from some other business, involving a Basque separatist group running hit-and-run terrorist operations from a base in the French Pyrenees and an arms shipment Dana had brokered. Vancouver had never actually met Dana, but he knew what the American looked like and what his business was—and he guessed that Melinda had something to do with it.

"He was in contact with a Palestinian group," Vancouver told her. "He had contracted with them to interrogate you. You wouldn't have been pretty afterward."

That seemed a waste, Vancouver said without irony—so Melinda wasn't sure if he referred to her mutilation, or Vince getting his hands on the information she possessed. Whichever, Vancouver decided he wanted her.

The easiest way to accomplish that was by killing Vince. He would kill her as quickly, if that became expedient.

But there was nothing to be done now, and no help in worrying about it. She did not want to die, but in the meantime . . .

She let her hand drift lower, circling the base of his semiturgid cock with her thumb and forefinger. "So," she said lightly, "what happened?" He had gone out no more than an hour earlier, without explanation, but she had managed to pry from the dull-witted Rook the information that he would return soon.

Vancouver turned his head slightly so he could see her face. "Three of the natives attacked me." His English was unaccented American, but it was toneless, without emotion or timber, almost like a computer-driven voice synthesizer.

Melinda began lazily to stroke him. "Why?"

"To kill me. I encourage them to try. I promise them money if they pull it off."

"You're offering a reward for your own corpse?" Melinda asked incredulously.

"No one has collected yet," Vancouver replied dryly. "It's a way of exercise."

"What happened to them?"

"I killed them."

Melinda's hand stopped moving. "I don't understand," she said in a small voice.

Vancouver looked at her for a long time without speaking, and Melinda had the uncomfortable feeling he was deciding whether giving her an explanation was worth the effort. "They lived on Socorro before I came here."

"When was that?"

Vancouver gave no indication of having heard. "Now they live under my protection because I find them convenient. Their presence gives the superficial impression that Socorro is merely some native island, and if a passerby tries to make landfall here, they . . . discourage him. If that doesn't work, they know other ways to dispose of visitors. Then there's the part where they help me train. . . ."

Melinda could not suppress a shudder.

"I've never hurt one of them unless I was attacked. They each know the reward and the risk."

"Death."

"Well, yes," Vancouver said. "Of course."

Psychology wasn't Melinda's field, but she knew enough of it to see that this was pathological. Vancouver was living under a sword of Damocles—by choice, for his own purposes.

Yet she had to admit: he had survived it so far.

She pulled away from him. Suddenly everything about Vancouver—his uninflected tone of voice, his depthless blue eyes, the unnaturalness of his posture as he lay on the bed beside her—all of it suggested death. His animation was false, contrived, the walking death of a zombie or a vampire.

"When are you going to kill me?" she asked levelly.

Vancouver looked at her. "I'm probably not," he answered, "although someone else might if you don't turn out to be useful. I'm going to sell you."

"To whom?"

"To whoever is willing to pay the most." Vancouver looked at the ceiling again. "You have some information that will command a great deal of money in some markets."

"Do I?" Melinda asked coolly.

"Certainly," Vancouver said, with absolute assurance. "For one example, you have been assigned a code number, a password, and a protocol for accessing the mainframe computer at the U.S. Department of Defense, because you are working on a routine analysis of twenty-year Defense spending. But because you have top security clearance, that same access allows you to tap many other data bases and files in the Defense computer. You could, for example, get a roster of embassy employees who are actually agents of Military Intelligence, handy information for a propagandist—or an assassin. For someone who wished to replenish his armory, and who did not mind a bit of hijacking, you could produce a listing of every shipment of U.S. armament during the next week worldwide. If a person was simply interested in causing chaos within the department and did not wish to go to a great deal of trouble, in a few hours at a terminal you could erase, rearrange, and distort enough data to cripple the system. It would take months to undo the damage you could cause."

Melinda Bannister kept her expression neutral. Vancouver's information was accurate in every detail. Either he had contacts with the intelligence service of some country antagonistic to the U.S., or a man of his own within the government. In any case he obviously had an extensive network.

"The numerical code, password, and protocol are changed every two weeks," Melinda said.

"I know that. I also know that you were assigned a new set ten days ago. Even though you were leaving on vacation, you were required to memorize them—that is S.O.P., and we both know the bureaucracy is a stickler for S.O.P. The set is good for four more days." His voice turned a few degrees more chill. "Whoever acquires you will take no more than four hours to find out what they want to know. I can guarantee that."

"Who will that be?" Melinda asked, working to keep the fear out of her tone.

Vancouver shrugged. "The computer code, as well as other, less perishable information, could be valuable to many nations, and several independent groups."

"Terrorists."

"That is correct. Tomorrow at midday, there will be an auction, conducted by radio. You are the only lot."

Melinda stared at him. "And then what?"

"I don't know. I'll be done with you. They'll probably start by asking you questions. What happens after that depends on your answers."

For some reason she was not as frightened as she should have been. Perhaps because it was all too dreamlike—she recalled again the miasma of thoughts that had possessed her like demons during her orgasms. It had moved too quickly: from unconsciousness on the Mediterranean beach to wakefulness and a headache in this place; she was not even sure where Socorro was located. She felt unmoored, floating a few feet above reality.

"There are men coming," Vancouver said suddenly.

"The men who are going to bid for me?"

"No." Vancouver's smile was faint and icy. "These men are coming to save you."

"But you're not going to let them."

"Of course not. I'm going to kill them."

"What if they make it?"

"They won't."

"What if it looks like they might? Will you kill me then?"

"No," Vancouver said. "I'll kill them."

He rolled over suddenly, and Melinda felt his hardness press into her thigh. Her skin felt chilled, a little damp. Vancouver began to move lower on her, but when she grabbed his hard shoulders he immediately stopped.

He had never forced her. She had the feeling he would not have come to her at all if she had not come to him first. She wondered why she had made this happen, if she should feel soiled or tainted by her own demands. But she did not and would not pretend to be for the sake of other people's preconceptions.

"Yes?" Vancouver said politely.

She opened her legs wider and moved her butt to adjust her position, drawing him back up and his mouth atop hers, and when he parted her and his length slid up into her she could not suppress the sounds of her need.

Chapter Twelve

"What the hell . . ." Conte said. He passed the binoculars to Ferdinand, but the other man waved them aside.

"I can see them all right; squinting across the sea strengthens a man's sight," Ferdinand said. "Negritos," he added.

Conte lay flat on his stomach on the built-up deck of the outrigger, and Ferdinand was crouched down in the hull beside him. They had taken down the mast to lower the boat's profile, and circled around to come in from the west, so the bright obscuring glare of the setting sun was at their backs.

"They are related to the Pygmies of Africa," Ferdinand said, "but they are native to this part of the Pacific. There are only about thirty thousand of them left in the Philippines, and most of them live on the out-islands. Usually they keep to themselves and live much as they have for millennia."

"Vancouver's guard force?" Conte asked skeptically. "What about the Moros?"

Ferdinand shrugged. Moros had been on their minds since they'd cleared the southern tip of the island of Negros. That put them into the heart of Moro territory; the big island of Mindanao, as well as Jolo, Tawitawi, and the dozens of smaller islands of the Sulu Archipelago, were either controlled by the Moros or sites of frequent violent attacks by the Muslimites in the name of conversion. To reduce the possibility of chance encounter, they provisioned up at Siaton and headed for open sea, staying out of identification range of the few fishing boats they encountered.

"Apparently he does not completely trust the Moros after all," Ferdinand guessed. "The Moros care for Islam more than life, and they will eventually turn on anyone who is not of the true faith. For the people he must share his island with, perhaps this Vancouver preferred the Pygmies."

Conte stared through the glasses. He counted six of them on the beach, about two miles from where the outrigger rode the gentle swell. They wore only loincloths, and they were heading south along the coast, as if on some kind of sentry patrol. Aside from knives, none of them seemed to be armed.

But then the cluster of the small dark men thinned out a little, and Conte saw that one of them was carrying something more lethal than a knife: an automatic rifle. From the shape of the banana clip, it was a Russian Kalashnikov, and in the hands of the Pygmy it looked outsized, as if someone had drawn the blueprints to the wrong scale.

"A security patrol," Conte suggested.

"Perhaps," Ferdinand murmured. "If so . . ."

"It means we're expected."

"Or someone else whom Vancouver does not wish to see."

"Let's figure the reception committee is in our honor," Conte said. "Better safe than sorry."

Earlier that day, from off Zamboanga at the southwest tip of Mindanao's panhandle, they had set a course almost due west, sighting the Pangutaran Group of islands about an hour earlier. From there they tacked north—and with each passing mile Conte felt more tense, as the nagging suspicion that the son-of-a-bitch Batu had lied about Socorro's location grew.

Once they left the Pangutarans behind, the open water of the Sulu Sea, sheltered by the surrounding ring of islands, was a nearly flat sheet of uniform azure. For an hour they saw nothing but sea birds, and by then they were north of the primary sea-lanes. According to the charts, there was no landfall for another two hundred miles. Conte's stomach was beginning to gnaw on itself when Ferdinand pointed and said, "There."

Conte followed the gesture, but he saw nothing until he unpacked the binocs, and then spotted only a slight imperfection in the otherwise flat line of the northern horizon. They had gone maybe another two miles but were still well out from it when they dropped sail, took down the mast, and began a circumnavigation for a preliminary surveillance of the island's features.

It was about a mile and a half long but only five or six hundred yards wide, shaped in a gently curving crescent. There was no reef as far as they could tell; most of the shore was white sand beach, except for a mangrove swamp at the southern end. The interior was mostly molave forest, beginning at the foot of a steep slope that rose perhaps two hundred feet and then leveled into a plateau, but there were also *cogonales* where the forest had been burned off for cultivation, then left to deteriorate into the coarse grass cover. In several places along the beach, spring-fed streams flowed down into the ocean.

It was after they had completed the full circuit and were lying at anchor that Conte spotted the Negritos on the beach.

He lowered the glasses. "Listen," he said carefully. "It could be this is exactly what it looks like: an isolated island inhabited by Pygmies. Vancouver could have nothing to do with any of this. He could be on another island, or another continent."

Ferdinand was burrowing in the crawl space below the built-up deck. Conte heard the rattle of tools and parts and whatever else was jumbled under there being pushed to one side, then the scraping of metal on wood as Ferdinand backed out, dragging a small chest.

"Just in case we are correct after all," Ferdinand said with a faint smile, "we had best be prepared."

He dug out a heavy ring of keys, used one on the chest's padlock, pushed back the lid. "I was able to find what you wished, and there are a few items here I keep on hand as well. Manila is a fine city for guns if a man knows where to shop."

Conte peered over Ferdinand's shoulder. The metal chest was lined with heavy-gauge plastic to protect the contents from the constant humidity. Ferdinand dug out a compact boxy handgun and passed it up to Conte. It was an Ingram M-11, per Conte's order, a 9 mm machine pistol no bigger than Conte's .45 automatic, but with a cyclic rate that sprayed off the lethal contents of its thirty-round magazine in less than two seconds. Conte dropped the magazine out of the handle grip, pulled back the cocking handle and checked the action, then unfolded the wire stock and made certain it seated correctly before folding it back up over the receiver again. It would do, he thought; it would do just fine.

Ferdinand was unpacking the rest of the chest's contents: a second Ingram, two of the new model AKM Soviet assault rifles chambered for 7.62 mm, and a dozen loaded magazines. For the Kalashnikovs there were the standard thirty-round banana clips, but for the Ingrams, Ferdinand had rigged up speedloads, two thirty-round sticks duct-taped butt to butt. Besides reducing reload time to a couple of seconds, the extra weight of the clip and ammo helped compensate against the potent little autogun's natural muzzle climb, up and to the left.

"Looks like we're prepared, all right," Conte murmured. "Now all we need is Vancouver, and we've got ourselves a party. If he's not on that damn island, we've gone to a lot of trouble for nothing."

Staying low, Ferdinand duckwalked back to the motor. "There is one way to find out," he said, and turned them back toward open sea.

Chapter Thirteen

"Conte, my friend," Ferdinand said, "you must understand. I know this country, these islands and how to move about on them. I can speak Tagalog and a little bit of the Negrito tongue, so that if we can get one of them aside, we may learn much—but only through me. I cannot in my conscience fail to accompany you."

Conte scowled in the darkness. The play was picking up speed now, barreling on toward showdown: in his gut Conte knew that Vancouver was somewhere on that island, and that the killer either held Melinda Bannister or knew where she was.

Men would die in twisted violent ways this night.

Conte would not be one of them, and he did not want to see Ferdinand hurt either. That's why he had tried to convince him one final time to stay shipboard. He knew it would do no good, but dammit, the neutralization of the assassin Vancouver was his mission, his risk. Sure, Conte knew Ferdinand could take care of himself, but if anything happened Conte would have to take the ultimate responsibility. Already Ferdinand had suffered a grievous loss. . . .

"There's Cilla, too," Conte said softly.

Ferdinand gave him a sharp look, which Conte met. It had to be said aloud; if Ferdinand was coming along, he had to control his compulsion to avenge the woman. Ferdinand would have his retribution—both men would see to that—but from this moment on, the foremost consideration had to be victory and survival, against nearly overwhelming and supremely deadly opposition.

"Yes," Ferdinand said finally, "there is my daughter. For what was done to her, Vancouver must pay—and he must make his payment to me and no other. First we will see to the woman you seek, I promise you this. But once that is done . . ." He stared out over the flat ocean toward the island. "Enough talk," he said gruffly. "There is much to be done on this night."

Conte climbed down from the deck and the two men began to rig up. By his Rolex it was two hours past midnight. The moon was a waning apostrophe hanging low in the western sky; within fifteen minutes it would dip below the horizon, and the next evening it would be new. But the night sky was cloudless, and the canopy of stars cast a dim glow on the mirror surface of the mile of water that separated the outrigger from the mangrove swamp at Socorro's southern tip. Since the patrol of Negritos had passed that afternoon, they had spotted no one else. Four miles offshore, they lay at anchor and took a light dinner, and after sundown Conte had managed to catch a few hours of sleep. As near as he could tell, Ferdinand had gone without again. There was something almost mystic about the big middle-aged man's strength and stamina, as if he were able to operate on adrenaline and determination if food and rest were in short supply.

Conte took off his windbreaker, unstrapped the shoulder holster under it, and removed his tennis shoes, which left him in slacks and T-shirt. He wrapped the .45 and its rig inside the jacket, baling it into a tight roll before swathing it in several layers of the heavy-gauge plastic sheeting. The bundle went into a dark rubber billybag with a double-fold Velcro seal, along with the tennis shoes, one of the Ingram

M-11s, two speedloader magazines, the Zippo, and three packs of Camels. The billybag in turn went into a web-cloth pack harness with two shoulder straps and a waist belt. Conte shrugged into it and adjusted the buckles.

Ferdinand strapped on his own pack, flashed Conte a thumbs-up and a tight grin, and went over the side. Conte breathed sweet night air into his lungs and followed.

The ocean was warm as mother's milk and smooth as a backyard pool, but the pack on Conte's back added a good twenty pounds to his weight. Ahead of him, Ferdinand swam like a machine, massive arms cutting smoothly and soundlessly through the dark water, legs pumping like a mechanical treadle.

The swim took Conte nearly forty-five minutes; twice he had to stop and tread water to catch his breath, and when he crawled up on the sandy beach his arms were numb, his legs leaden, and his lungs seared. They had made landfall at the edge of the mangrove swamp, on a stretch of open shore about twenty yards wide, abutted by the forest. Ferdinand was waiting patiently inside the cover of the tree line, sitting with his back against the trunk of a kamagong. Conte managed to unstrap his pack—which seemed to have taken on quite a bit more weight in the course of the swim—and drag it up to where Ferdinand blended into the shadows, before flopping over on his back to wait for his heartbeat to drop toward normal again.

It took five minutes, but by then the blood had returned to his limbs and the coolness of the night breeze wicking the seawater from his clothing and skin perked him up. Conte sat up and said, "Let's get moving," in a low voice, and Ferdinand began to work on the fasteners of his billybag.

The contents of Conte's pack had come through without seawater penetrating. He strapped on the shoulder rig, jacked a cartridge into the chamber of the .45, and seated it in its accustomed spot. This was habit; Conte had carried the Colt for all of his violent adult life, and he felt unbalanced if the automatic was not in place. The windbreaker went over it; Conte zipped the jacket halfway up and transferred the Zippo and cigarettes to the pockets. In the bottom of the billybag there was a leather thong with a loop in one end and a snapbolt in the other; Conte connected the ends, slipped the lanyard over his head, and fastened the snapbolt to an eyebolt in the top of the Ingram's frame.

Ferdinand gathered up the pack frames and the billybags and disappeared into the forest. When he returned empty-handed thirty seconds later, Conte was tying the laces of his tennis shoes. He straightened and nodded. Ferdinand, the M-11 looking like a toy in his big mitt, turned and led the way into the thick rain-forest foliage.

Within the trees it was shadowy and much darker, so that Conte could not see Ferdinand if the big brown man got more than a few steps ahead. The molave, the hardwood ipil, and the red narra were deciduous trees, many of them rising as high as a hundred feet to form a broad-leafed canopy over the forest floor. Ferns rustled around his legs as Conte pressed forward up the slope toward the island's crest. From there they could figure out some kind of systematic recon.

Something dark flashed by, not more than a few feet from Conte's face, and instinctively he grabbed the stock and grip of the Ingram and dropped to one knee, tracking to his left as the black projectile plunged into an atis bush scattering leaves. He flicked the selector to full auto, his finger tautening on the trigger.

"Bat." Ferdinand materialized at Conte's side. "You find them everywhere in the islands at night."

Conte slowly unwound his fingers from the Ingram and

rose, tucking it back inside the windbreaker where it hung from the leather lanyard. *Only a bat,* he thought.

And Vancouver was only a man.

"Are you all right, friend Conte?" Ferdinand whispered.

"Better than ever." Conte checked the luminous dial of the Rolex: past three in the morning. "Let's go."

Fifty yards further on Conte caught the silhouette of a monkey, the flash of its tail immediately disappearing among the branches overhead. They passed through a copse of wild cane growing on the slope side, and in this semiclearing the sudden brilliance of the starlight after the forest's blackness was startling.

Beyond the cane the hillside steepened perceptibly, and away from the salt-laden sea breeze the trees grew closer together and the underbrush thickened. A few yards in front of him, Conte could hear Ferdinand's thick legs swish through the ferns and low bushes, but the darkness had closed in on them again, and he could not see past the next stringy-barked tree trunk. They had come maybe a half mile, Conte guessed, without striking any further sign of the Negritos, any indication of habitation at all, but instinct told Conte they had come to the right place. Or maybe he was just impatient. The mission had taken him halfway around the world in a few days, and he wanted it to end— successfully—here, in this place on this night.

Conte pulled up abruptly. He had been daydreaming and suddenly had no sense of the trail he was following. It struck him that the rain forest had gone dead silent: no rustle of leaves, no animal sounds, no flutter of bat wings.

No noise of Ferdinand, a few yards in the lead.

Conte dug out the Ingram and called his partner's name in a harsh whisper.

That was when the Negrito dropped out of the trees.

The Negrito landed on his shoulders, and the impact drove Conte two steps forward. He would have gone down if he hadn't steadied himself against a molave, but by then the little bastard had both forearms locked around his throat and was kicking at Conte's ribs with both heels.

Conte bent at the waist and threw his weight forward, and the Pygmy grunted and lost his grip and flipped over Conte's head, landing hard on his back. Conte sidestepped away and tracked the Ingram onto the guy's chest, thumbing the selector from safety to semiauto. He didn't want to lose the guy, but he wanted to put him down, and quick. The forest was the Negrito's territory, and Conte didn't want to give him the home-court advantage in a game of cat-and-mouse.

The Negrito stood and drew a knife from his loincloth, the twelve-inch blade shiny even in the forest darkness. He was thin and wiry looking, with frizzy hair and a prognathous jaw like a third fist. Although he came up maybe to Conte's breastbone, he looked dangerous as hell.

Conte hesitated. He needed the bastard alive, and besides, he wanted to avoid the noise of gunfire if possible.

Then the Negrito crouched and charged, the knife held blade-up for slashing and swishing through the air in a smooth sweep. Conte sidestepped and the tip of the honed steel missed his abdomen by maybe an inch, and still he did not fire.

But the Negrito's arm swung back in the same effortless motion, and Conte felt the shock of the impact as hard cold metal parted his soft flesh. There was the warm wetness of his own blood gushing out to soak his skin and run down his leg in itchy rivulets, for a moment no pain but only the certain, almost detached knowledge, that he had made a dangerous error.

Then combat instincts took over. The Negrito thrust the

blade full at Conte's chest, and Conte spun away, swinging the short barrel of the Ingram to catch the knifeman on the wrist. He heard the blade drop into the underbrush, but his own left leg was not working correctly and he could not keep his balance, and when he went down to his knees he felt the tearing agony for the first time.

Two yards away, the Negrito groveled among the ferns. He came up with the haft of the big knife in both hands, and lunged once more at Conte.

Conte shot him between his dark eyes, and at that range the disintegrating 9 mm jacketed slug hit like a fist thrown at 900 feet per second. A hole seemed to open at the bridge of the Pygmy's broad flat nose and the rest of his face collapsed into it as the man fell away to one side. The noise of the Ingram's report echoed among the trees and faded to the same unnatural silence that had preceded the attack.

Conte tried to stand, and moaned with the pain. Leaving the Ingram to hang from its lanyard, he used both hands and the good leg to drag himself a few feet to where he could get his back against the trunk of a molave. The front of his slacks over his left thigh was heavy with his blood, and he could feel more oozing from the wound. With each pulse beat there was a sympathetic throb of sharp ache. The tear in the twill material of his pants was horizontal, and from the way the leg would not respond correctly, tendons had been slashed. That and the amount of blood meant the cut was deep and serious. It was only a matter of time before he went into shock, and after that, blood infection was a certainty unless he got the wound cleaned and treated.

Vancouver would have to wait. Right now he had to find Ferdinand and get the hell off this goddamned island. Dead, he was no good to anyone.

And dead was starting to look like a distinct possibility.

There were a half dozen of them, standing over him in a semicircle with a radius of three feet and Conte at the hub. Their primitive-looking features were inscrutable masks that at his moment projected to Conte great menace.

Three of them drew knives.

Conte brought up the Ingram and threw the selector forward to full autofire. The machine pistol was heavier and so were his arms, and it was an effort to lift them, and the time for fucking around was long past. Conte threw down on the end man and squeezed the Ingram's tigger.

Before the hammer fell—a fraction of a second before, it seemed to Conte—someone screamed, an eerie animal jungle cry. An eight-shot burst cut into the foliage before Conte could release, but none of the six Pygmies went down. They were gone, melted into the jungle like dreams at dawn.

Conte drew a deep ragged breath. He dug his folding knife from his pocket, but his fingers felt cold and were going numb, and it took three tries before he could worry the blade open. He used it to lengthen the tear in his pant leg, gingerly picking the bloody cotton away from his skin.

The wound looked as bad as it felt. It ran parallel to his waist for a good four inches across the meaty part of his thigh, two-thirds of the way up from the knee. It was deep enough so the puckered edges of severed skin were pulled apart by muscle tension, and he could see down into his own bloody meat nearly an inch.

Conte gulped back a wave of nausea. His face was soaked with sweat at the same time a chill shiver racked his torso. He leaned his head back against the tree trunk's support and drew deep breaths, counting beats in his mind to force steady aspiration and the revivification brought by mild hyperventilation.

When he was breathing steadily on his own, he used

the knife and his fingers to rip the torn pant leg completely away; drops of his blood flew from it as it jerked free. He grappled above his head for a low branch, then remembered there were none, and he had to drag himself away from the tree to find a deadfall stick big enough to serve in a tourniquet. He wrapped a strip of material from the pant leg around his thigh below his crotch, then knotted it loosely around the stick. When he twisted it to inhibit the blood flow to the limb, the wound responded with a sharp stab of pain, but by the time he managed to reknot the cloth to hold the tourniquet firm, it had ebbed to a constant throbbing ache.

The jungle was quiet as a crypt.

"Ferdinand." He meant to whisper, but the sound came out sharp and raspy, like someone else's voice. Conte tried it again and it sounded no more natural.

The silence closed in again like a shroud.

It took him several minutes to pull himself erect. His left leg would not bend correctly, but it mostly held his weight. Brush whipped at his face as he limped off in the direction he thought Ferdinand had been heading. He called the name a third time, and still there was no answer.

Ten yards further on, Conte found out why.

Ferdinand lay facedown in a tiny clearing, and the crushed ferns sticking out from under his massive torso were stained with his blood. His arms were flung outward and his face was pressed into the ground.

Conte drew a deep breath and knelt beside his friend. He got both hands around Ferdinand's shoulder and biceps, grunting with the pain and effort of flipping his body.

Conte gasped and stumbled away, his hands smeared with Ferdinand's blood. Where his friend's face should have been there was a gory mask of bloody mutilated flesh with shards of greasy white skull bone shining through. A knife blade had been drawn from the base of Ferdinand's neck to below his navel, and gray-blue ropes of entrails hung obscenely from the slit.

The bastards had gone out of their way to slash his flesh to strips of dead meat, and what was left only vaguely resembled a man.

On top of Conte's pain and incipient shock, this was more than he could take. He barely managed to roll over and prop himself up on his hands before vomit spewed from his mouth. He retched out the food they had taken hours before, and when that was gone he retched bile, and then he retched dry spasms of nothing at all.

When it stopped, he crawled away from the mess—the one of his own making, and the one that had been Ferdinand—and lay on his back in the ferns listening to his heart pound and feeling the dank sweat chill his skin, and if they had come upon him then, he would not have raised a hand in defense of his life.

The Rolex told Conte he had been out for fifteen minutes; he would have guessed several hours. He still felt weak as a child, and the chills were shuddering across his body beyond any possibility of control, but the pain in his leg was barely noticeable, masked by an almost sensual numbness.

Conte sat up with a start and clawed at the tourniquet with stiff fingers. Sure the leg was numb; the blood flow to it was cut to a trickle.

He got the cloth loose and untwisted the stick, then massaged at the thigh until he felt the first tingling twinges of pain returning. The bleeding started up again, but it was down to a slow ooze. Conte swore under his breath; if he did not loosen the tourniquet periodically, gangrene would set in and he would lose the leg. He imagined himself like that, nothing below his left side but an empty hip socket, hobbling around on crutches waiting for the other leg to atrophy, and men's pitying stares focused on him wherever he went, stabbing into him like a constant torment of pinpricks.

Conte shook the image out of his mind. But he was all right now, calm enough at least to do what had to be done. Loosening the tourniquet, remembering that survival counted above all, seemed to set him back on track.

Nausea did not return when he flipped Ferdinand back on his stomach. Conte felt only emptiness at his new friend's death; mourning, responsibility, and other useless emotions would have to wait for another time. The fanny pack he had been wearing was still strapped to the back of Ferdinand's waist; Conte had to wipe slippery blood from the zipper handle before he could work it open. Inside he found three protein bars wrapped in foil, two pieces of the dried squid, a plastic pint bottle of water, a Buck knife, a spool of monofilament fishline, and a plastic kit twice the size of a cigarette pack with a red cross on the front. He started to unstrap the pack, then reconsidered and simply stuffed the items into the pockets of his windbreaker and his torn slacks. Ferdinand's Ingram was wedged under his torso, and it took a moment for Conte to pry it free. He dropped the magazine out of the receiver and threw it into the darkness as hard as he could. He heard it thump into a tree trunk over his own grunt of pain. He took the unloaded machine pistol and stabbed the muzzle into the ground, twisting it like a drill bit until he was sure dirt was jammed up the barrel all the way back to the chamber, then threw it in the opposite direction.

It was nearly four in the morning when he reached the top of the slope. He was not sure if it was the crest they had seen from the water, and did not particularly care. For this night he was done moving; he had no more strength to tap. The hilltop was mostly bare, except for a thick-foliaged flat-leaved banana tree. Conte flopped to the ground, ignoring his leg's spasm of protest as he dragged himself up against the trunk.

Somewhere on the edge of his subconscious, he knew what deep trouble he was in. Logic told him he was alone against a force of men—he did not even know how many. Logic told him he was wounded so badly he might become completely incapacitated within hours. Logic told him he was on alien ground without support, allies, shelter, or a plan.

Logic told him he was a dead man.

But logic was not going to help him now, and Conte refused to let any of those thoughts escape into full consciousness. Logic was one thing, but reason was another. Reason told him that survival was everything now, and survival came one step at a time.

The first step was the leg wound. In the medical kit he found bandages, aspirin, a four-ounce bottle of alcohol, a vial of five-hundred-milligram penicillin tablets, another of five-mil Dexedrine, and a suture and nylon thread. He swallowed ten of the antibiotic pills, four of the aspirin, and two of the Dexedrine, washing them down two at a time. He tried to take shallow sips from the water bottle, but suddenly he was uncontrollably thirsty, and when he lowered it, the bottle was empty. He had been sweating constantly, and he realized that he had been—likely still was—badly dehydrated. At that moment a wave of cramps constricted his stomach like a mailed fist. Conte gulped air and swallowed; it took a concentration of will, but in the end he managed to keep the water and the medication down.

Stitching the wound was another story.

He did not have enough will to force himself to stare

down through the gash; only the sure knowledge that if he
did not close it he would die from the blood loss enabled
him to do what he had to. He squeezed the torn edges of
skin together with the thumb and forefinger of his left hand,
held the curved suture in his right. He breathed deeply, let
out half the breath and held the rest—as if he were about to
make a long and difficult rifle shot, he thought irrelevant-
ly—and pushed the sharp point in one side of the puckered
ridge of flesh, firm and steady, until enough of the thin barb
of metal emerged from the other side for him to grasp. The
pain was not unbearable, but the shock and the eerie feeling
of sewing up his own flesh combined to palsy his hands. He
had to pause four times until deep breathing steadied him
again.

But each time the chills became more intense, more
difficult to subdue, and when he had taken fifteen stitches
and the mouth of the wound was an uneven crooked line
crisscrossed with thread, he was on the brink of losing it
completely once more. He tilted up the water bottle, and a
thin trickle, half a mouthful in all, went down his parched
throat. His face was soaked with sweat cold as ice water,
and his nervous system would no longer control his
muscles. Somehow he remembered the tourniquet: now that
he was stitched up he did not need it anymore.

He got the knot undone and saw the two ends of the
cloth fall loose and away, before the pain and the chills and
the numbness and the delirium all were swallowed whole by
a maw of absolute blackness.

Chapter Fourteen

Melinda Bannister stretched out one long perfectly formed leg and began to apply a thin layer of tanning oil. She started at her ankle, working the soothing balm into her soft skin, moved up to massage her calf, then above the knee to the expanse of thigh exposed by the high-cut bikini bottom, working around the hem of the suit to the vee of the little swath of white spandex around her loins. Already her skin was tanned the uniform color of light caramel, and in vivid contrast her naturally pale blond mane was bleached platinum. Melinda ran her fingers along the thin skin at the inside of her thighs; the fine down there was also bleached. A single tendril of blond pubic hair descended from under the elasticized band of the bikini. She twined it around her little finger.

So when the rough voice behind her said, "Food, Lady," Melinda was a little startled and sat up in the chaise lounge primly, like an adolescent boy suddenly afraid his palms would grow hair.

The Negrito woman carried a round tray holding a covered dish, silverware, a tapa-cloth napkin, two white china cups, and a tall aluminum pot of coffee with a black plastic top. Her name was Eula, and she kept her head down and her eyes averted from Melinda when she set the tray on the table. In height she came up to Melinda's nipples; her tight black hair was cut short, like a furry skullcap, and her dark wide eyes framed a spatulate nose with flaring nostrils that added to what appeared to be a facial expression of constant disapproval. She wore a tapa-cloth skirt and nothing else; her breasts were small, but they sagged like the paps of a nursing bitch.

She poured coffee, then removed the cover from the dish. "Fried egg," she recited, staring down as if addressing the meal in question. "Spice-beef and *kutsinta*." She risked a quick glance at Melinda. "Is rice cake," she explained.

Melinda adjusted the top of the bikini, which consisted of a thin band of matching white spandex that did nothing for her full breasts except draw attention to them. Although it was only two hours past dawn, the sun was already high in the eastern sky; here, less than seven degrees north of the equator, it rose quickly and dominated the day relentlessly. Melinda felt a single pearl of sweat roll down into the deep valley between her breasts as she pulled herself out of the chaise lounge and glided to the round umbrella-shaded table where Eula was setting out her meal.

The Negrito woman's eyes were studiously averted as Melinda sat down. The chair was wrought metal and felt chill for a moment against Melinda's shoulder blades and the backs of her thighs. The Negrito nodded at the ground and had started to turn away when Melinda spoke her name. Eula stopped and stared at the flat beach stones caulked with packed sand from which the patio behind Vancouver's open house was fashioned.

Melinda regarded the short dark woman with curiosity. She felt there was something she wanted to ask, but was not sure what. "Sit down, Eula."

"Oh, no, Lady."

"Why not?" Melinda was vaguely amused. She picked up the rice cake and nibbled at the edge, watching the Negrito.

"Not nice."

"To sit with me?" Perhaps the woman was afraid of Vancouver. "Don't worry. I promise you won't get in trouble."

Eula shook her head vigorously. "No, no, no, Lady." She finally looked up, blinking at her frustration in communicating. She swept both hands down the length of her body, then gestured at Melinda. "Not nice," she repeated, then quickly apologized: "Sorry to say, Lady."

Melinda stared uncomprehendingly—then burst into laughter. Vancouver's Negrito maid was not afraid of being punished for fraternizing; she simply found Melinda, by her standards, hopelessly repulsive looking.

But at the sound of the laughter, Eula looked up, and her stern expression softened. "I'm sorry, too," Melinda said gently. "Please, Eula, sit down."

The Negrito woman glanced over her shoulder at the house, then slid into the chair opposite, her toes just touching the stone. "Eat, Lady," she said, like an anxious mother. "Is good."

Melinda carved off a piece of the spicy beef and dipped it in egg yolk. It was good, and suddenly she was hungry. The instinct for survival, she figured. . . .

Her fate would be decided this day, Vancouver had said. She was badly frightened, though she refused to show her fear. Part of it was subsumed by anger anyway—at him, certainly, but perhaps at herself as well—mostly at the damnable turns life could take.

The image of her husband Lawrence came suddenly and unbidden into the focus of her mind; she had not really thought of him since this had begun, with the gory murder of Vince on the beach at Monte Carlo. Was she in Lawrence's thoughts at this moment, she wondered? Seven years earlier BST had been involved in some experiments in parapsychology, and the results tended to confirm the validity of telepathy. She wondered now: was the ability to communicate by thought a function of love?

She was not sure if she loved her husband, because she was not sure what love meant. By other people's definition of the emotion, she supposed she did. She respected him: his brilliance, his success in his field and his business, his dedication to science and to his country. With her he was a tender, thoughtful man, and despite the turmoil and hurt and anger and recriminations that had become the routine of their marriage, he would not give her up. He constantly worked to build intimacy, like another husband might fashion a redwood picnic table. He encouraged her to come to him, and he listened. He came to her, boyish and almost apologetic, to tell her his concerns.

Mostly they had to do with her men.

She had married him because she thought it would change her; she could admit that now, though wryly and with some embarrassment at her youthful naïveté. Of course it had not: there had always been men before Lawrence, and there were always men afterward. She did not lie to him, and probably that made it worse for him. But ultimately there was this: she was not willing to change.

She was not a nymphomaniac, never promiscuous. She did not go home from cocktail lounges with nameless men, nor drag other women's husbands into the guest room at parties. Like the affair with Vince Dana, all of her relationships had been long-term. She had never fallen in love; if she was capable of that emotion as others defined it, it was only toward Lawrence. Years ago, he had offered to divorce her, and she had been startled; she had never wanted to commit to anyone but him.

"Eat," Eula said suddenly. The Negrito woman was watching her openly—now that she had managed her repulsion, Melinda thought with a wan smile. She took another bite of the breakfast, and nodded and murmured appreciatively. Eula smiled her dark smile.

It came down to this: she would not compromise. She was a brilliant scientist who had made vital contributions to the security and well-being of her country; she deserved her fun.

Yet the fun always had to include the thrill, the delicious *frisson* that only danger brought. Perhaps, she thought now, the need for the thrill had become pathological, addictive; perhaps, like a heroin user, she needed ever increasing doses to get a jolt.

Perhaps, like the addict, she had reached a wall and was about to burn out.

She had known that her affairs posed security risks; she and Lawrence had frankly discussed it. She was a private citizen employed by a private company, she insisted. Her personal life was her own, not her government's.

Now she knew that she was wrong, and the penalty for her error was going to be severe.

She was aware Vince was involved in industrial espionage, but she thought he was only stealing secrets from one company to sell to another, and she did not choose to let that concern her. She knew now that Vince had been a traitor, with the moral sense of a hyena. She took no satisfaction in his murder, but neither did she mourn him.

Right now, she had her own neck to worry about.

She knew the value of the information and intelligence she could provide. To an enemy of the U.S.—an unfriendly nation, a terrorist group—what she knew could provide significant leverage, possibly enough to tip the world balance. In their efforts to get her to talk, they would not be gentle. If she did not cooperate, she would die. Most likely she would die anyway.

A finger of terror tickled at her spine, and she willed

herself to ignore its touch. On this island with Vancouver she was hamstrung, but panic would not help. She had to stay calm, keep her eyes and ears open, and be ready to take advantage of any small break that against all odds might come her way.

"How did your people come to this place?" she asked.

Eula sat up, a little surprised by the sudden question. "Come long ago, Lady." She pointed upward. "From the sky."

It sounded like some kind of creation legend, so Melinda assumed the Negritos were native to this island.

"Him come from the sea," she went on, anticipating Melinda's question. "Not long ago not at all."

Melinda remembered the previous afternoon, Vancouver's frigid detached tone as he told her about the three Pygmies, their attack and their deaths. She was repulsed and fascinated.

"Why did you let him come here?" Melinda pressed.

Eula looked at the ground. "Scared, Lady." But then she brightened. "But much money."

"Those three who attacked him yesterday. Did he really kill them?"

"Oh, yes. Most of all money there."

"But they died."

"Most of all money, but most of all blood and death, too." Eula shook her head. "Maybe better for all if they kill him, but . . ." She frowned, searching for a way to express what she meant. "He is . . . knife or gun, he is . . ." She held her right palm stiff and made a slashing gesture with it across her left arm. "Pass through, and no blood at all."

They had elevated Vancouver to the supernatural; Melinda wondered how many Negritos had died during his grisly practice sessions before they began to see him as a demi-diety. There was something suprahuman about Vancouver: the kind of cold, mechanical perfection Melinda associated with technology. Yet there was an uncanny aura of extrasensory perception to him as well: the way he knew her body, and sometimes seemed to know her thoughts.

Whatever his powers, they were not enhanced by love.

"Now, though, maybe . . ." Eula said. "Maybe the other can do."

Melinda frowned. "What other?"

"Men come, Lady." She stabbed a stubby dark finger across the patio table. "Come for you, I think. You are . . ."

Her voice trailed off and she jumped from the metal seat as if it were suddenly red hot, jarring the tabletop hard enough to slop coffee from Melinda's cup. Melinda looked over her shoulder and saw Vancouver coming out of the house, trailed by the dull-witted *mestizo* bodyguard, Rook. Rook stopped at the edge of the patio and folded his massive arms, and stood glaring, as if he took the flawless tropical morning as a grave personal insult.

Vancouver looked over Melinda's body, methodically as a horseman rating a brood mare. His blue eyes were opaque as cut gemstones. They swept up over her flat stomach, the swell of her full breasts straining against the stretched cloth and the outline of her nipples, the long sweep of her neck. Finally he met her gaze; he seemed to be waiting for something.

"I'm finished, Eula," Melinda said.

The Negrito maid was relieved to be dismissed. She gathered up the remains of Melinda's breakfast with a clatter of dishes and flatware, and fled for the house.

Vancouver sat down in the chair she had abandoned. He poured coffee in the second cup but left it to steam in front of him. Melinda realized she had never seen him drink anything but water in the week she had been with him.

"You leave today," Vancouver said abruptly. "You'll want to be ready."

"Where am I going?"

Vancouver shrugged. "The auction is at noon."

"For me."

"That's right." He stared at her steadily, like a researcher observing a rat in a maze. She would not beg, so she sat and returned his look. It seemed very quiet on the patio.

Then Vancouver reached in the breast pocket of his polo shirt and removed a photograph. He dropped it on the grid of the table in front of Melinda.

The photograph was tinted an unnatural red and the foliage in the background was foreshortened from the effect of a telephoto lens. A man was lying on his side under a tree, sprawled in an unnatural position for sleep. One of his legs was bare and smeared with a lot of dried blood.

"Did you kill him?" she asked evenly.

"He isn't dead." Vancouver speared the picture with two fingers and regarded it. "Do you know him?"

"No." Vancouver's detachment made her guts clench. He might have been talking about a piece of sculpture.

"His name is Matthew Conte," Vancouver said. "He's a contract killer for American gangsters."

"You know him?"

"No. I know who he is. There are people who would pay a lot of money to have me killed, so I like to keep track of the people whom they might hire to do the job. There are not so many who can . . . handle the work."

He looked away, and the faintest hint of expression came into his finely chiseled face. Melinda recognized it and recoiled: nostalgia.

"Did he come for me?" she asked.

Vancouver looked at her. "That doesn't matter, does it? There was another man with him, a Filipino fisherman who had stuck his nose into other people's trouble before, but the Negritos killed him. They could have killed Conte, too. I told them not to."

"You knew they were on the island?"

"I knew they were coming," Vancouver corrected.

"Why did you save this man?"

"I don't know," Vancouver said, almost dreamily. From the patio a single wedge of the ocean below was visible through the surrounding forest, and now Vancouver studied it like a rune. "I thought . . ." He looked back to her. "Do I repel you now?"

Melinda tugged at the top of the bikini; it seemed too small and she felt exposed. "You frighten me."

"You'll recollect my touch with passion and loathing." He pronounced it like a malediction. He stared at the sliver of far-off sea once more. "They taught it to us all. I learned better than the others. I was always the best at it, because I saw its art and grace."

He smiled. He had not done that before. His smile was beatific, a smile of inner peace.

"I mean killing," he said.

"I know what you mean."

He stared at her for a long time, then nodded his head. Feet scraped stone, and Rook materialized at the side of the table. He stared at Melinda's breasts like a schoolboy at a stag movie.

Vancouver tapped the center of the photograph with a forefinger. "It's all right now," he said.

Rook grinned slackly and turned on his heel.

"There's nothing he could tell me." His tone was reasonable, as if he were explaining a new theory of social interaction. "He's badly hurt. There wouldn't be any point in my going after him."

"No challenge."

"Exactly." If he heard the cold sarcasm in her voice, he ignored it.

Melinda pushed back her chair. "I'm going to put on some clothes."

When she started to pass, he caught her wrist. He did not hurt her, but she knew somehow that he would not allow her to break free.

"You see now, don't you?" he said.

"Let me go please."

"Of course." His hand fell away.

She felt stiff and self-conscious as she walked toward the house, knowing he was watching her and feeling her bare skin prickle as his gaze passed over it. It seemed to generate heat, like a magnifying glass focusing the sun, and she felt it sear into the spot between her shoulders and beneath the nape of her neck, the spot directly over her heart.

Chapter Fifteen

Matt Conte awoke from feverish sleep, gasping and moaning and blinking back tears of rage and impotence. Ferdinand: the image of his dead partner came immediately with consciousness, vividly stomach wrenching. But that was mostly the Dexedrine playing its tricks; Conte concentrated on taking shallow regular breathes, and the vision left him. He became aware of the glare of the sun, already thirty degrees above the horizon; it was hitting him full in the face, and he squinted and ducked his head. He looked at the Rolex: it was just past eight. The ambush in the forest had happened less than five hours earlier.

First Cilla, and now Ferdinand; Conte swore, and the anger seemed to revive him. Then, as blood began to flow more freely into his sleep-numbed limbs, the pain resumed its thumping pulse beat in the upper part of his leg, and Conte remembered how deep a hole he was in.

He found a protein bar in his jacket pocket and stripped off the foil, but when he bit off a piece his mouth was so dry he could barely chew. He forced his jaws to work while he examined the gash in his leg. The stitching had held, and there were no white patches or striated vessels further down on the limb to indicate gangrene or advanced blood poisoning, but there was a livid redness around the wound itself to confirm that the inevitable infection had set in. Conte found the vial of penicillin in another pocket and chewed up six tablets with the protein bar.

When he had managed to get all of it masticated and

swallowed, Conte dug a crumpled pack of Camels and the Zippo from his pants pocket. The cigarettes were bent and discolored from the dampness, but a couple were unbroken. Conte smoked and forced his mind to focus.

He was in a world of trouble, and there were not a hell of a lot of options open to him.

Even if he could make it down to the shore unmolested, there was no way off the island; if he tried to swim, he'd drown before he got halfway to the boat. But if he stayed where he was, he'd die from the wound—if Vancouver or one of his Pygmy pals didn't get him first.

So he couldn't go backward and he couldn't stay put—which left one path out of this mess.

Right through Vancouver's goddamned front door.

He quick-checked the Ingram, then worked the action of the automatic. There was nothing wrong with either gun. Now, if he only had two good legs and a half-dozen men fighting next to him. . . .

Conte shook his head, impatient with himself. There was no point in maundering fantasies. He was alone and hurt, and he'd have to make do, or die.

Matt Conte did not plan to die.

His bad leg mostly supported his weight when he stood, but walking on it took too much concentration and cost too much pain. He used Ferdinand's Buck knife on a green limb of a kamagong at the edge of the hilltop clearing. Fifteen minutes later he was soaked with sweat from the exertion and from fever, but he had managed to fashion a serviceable crutch.

He studied the terrain for several minutes before he made out the edge of the mangrove swamp below, and that landmark plus the position of the sun told him they had come from that direction the night before, from the south.

In the other direction the island stretched for perhaps a mile; he could see the ocean on either side and the white beach along its rim, but the view due north was blocked by another hilltop, rising seventy or eighty feet above his position. The crest was perhaps a half mile overland, and the texture of the treetops seemed to drop off around it—a clearing? Conte wondered. High ground was the most likely place for Vancouver's base.

The effort of cutting the crutch had reawakened his dehydration, and by the time he had bushwhacked a hundred yards through the forest his thirst had become a desperate all-consuming obsession, strong enough to block the pain of his leg. He could not afford the preoccupation. He had to be alert, to concentrate; there were men on this island who wanted him dead, and any bush might hide them.

He moved a half-dozen steps at a time, silently as Ferdinand, pausing to recon his path and double-check his back track before moving on. He did not notice when the molave woods gave way to a deep stand of bamboo, and was cursing himself at having literally missed the forest for the trees—and right then was when he almost tripped over the two Negritos.

He whipped up the Ingram, thumbed the selector to full auto, and thought savagely, *the hell with the noise*. Maybe letting Vancouver find him was the only way to force a showdown before the leg wound incapacitated him beyond hope of survival.

But the Negrito man took two quick steps backward and threw up his hands, and Conte held fire. The Negrito man looked younger than the others, as did the woman cowered at his side. The man was holding a machete, but hanging down at his side as if he had forgotten about it; he had been chopping bamboo and had already built up a small pile.

Beside the pile was a skin bag.

Conte pointed, then opened his parched lips and croaked, "Water."

The Negrito couple stared at him woodenly.

Conte cupped his hands and raised them to his lips, miming drinking.

The Negrito man nodded vigorously. He picked up the skin bag and held it out, edging warily closer. Conte realized he was still pointing the Ingram at the man, and sheepishly lowered the weapon. So not all of the Negritos belonged to Vancouver's private army. . . .

The water was tepid and had a greasy taste, but to Conte it was sweet as life. He forced himself to swallow a mouthful at a time, pausing after several gulps to let the water settle on his stomach. When he was sure it would stay down, he drank again. The Negritos watched with something like fascination, as if he were a benign representative of another galaxy.

"Do you speak English?" Conte's voice sounded more normal. The Pygmies stared back. *Dammit,* Conte thought; he had the edge almost in grasp. If he could only figure out some way to communicate. . . .

"The other man," he said. He pointed at his face, then held out a hand, palm down at about his own height. If Vancouver was six six and black, the gesture wouldn't mean much.

But the Negrito man nodded vigorously—and pointed to his wife. Conte stared at him. The Negrito grabbed the woman's bare breast and held it out toward Conte, like an offering.

Then he got it. "A white woman? There's a white woman with him?"

But the Negrito was looking at Conte, an expression of stark fear blooming on his face. Instinctive reaction powered Conte's dive to one side, his hands grabbing for the Ingram as he rolled over in the undergrowth. A burst of autofire tore through the space he had occupied a fraction of a second earlier.

He saw the bulk of a man among the thick green stalks of bamboo, perhaps twenty yards away—and then he caught sight of the dark swarthy scowl flavored with Oriental features, and felt a jolt of adrenaline pummel his heart like an electric current. Rook, his and Kay's playmate in the Belgrade soccer stadium: if he was here, so was Vancouver.

Conte put a six-shot burst in Rook's direction, more to pin him down than to do any real damage. Rook had the advantage of mobility, but he had given some weight by blowing the ambush. The play now was to keep him pinned down until there was a clear shot.

The bamboo stalks were mature, the hollow, pale green trunks as large as eighteen inches across, the foliage leaves over a hundred feet above them. They grew thick enough to keep a man on the run from cutting a straight trail, but aside from a few sparse bushes there was little undergrowth. The sameness of the stalks was disorienting to Conte; it was like fighting in a maze.

He began to knee-and-elbow from his position, and found what was left of the Negrito couple.

Rook's burst from the AKM assault rifle had stitched across them at chest level. The woman lay on her back, blood smeared across her bare chest and puddled on her stomach, and the man lay curled on his side and half atop her, so Conte could count the line of four angry red exit wounds equally spaced from shoulder to shoulder.

Conte moved out in the other direction, ears straining

for the sound of Rook's movement, eyes scanning the thick stand of bamboo. He caught the glint of gunmetal and hit the dirt again, but Rook was aiming five yards from Conte's position. The bastard was hazing him more deeply into the bamboo, where the growth was most thick. Conte tossed the makeshift crutch aside, clutched the Ingram to his chest with his right hand, used his left on the tree trunks for support as he moved within them.

In the corner of his eye Conte saw movement, and he tracked the gun around. Rook wore cammie trousers, a machete in a belt sheath, and nothing else; that registered before Conte fired, and by then the big man had disappeared into the bamboo again.

Conte went down and crawled in the same direction. The AKM ratcheted from somewhere within the bamboo and a swarm of slugs buzzed angrily over Conte's head. He counted a beat and cautiously raised his head, but there was only a broken wall of green stalks, the tree-sized grass almost as thick as some kind of monstrous lawn.

The pain in Conte's leg was sharpening again, and when he checked the wound, he saw blood oozing between the stitches. The Dexedrine was starting to let him down again, but that didn't matter because the fever was making his mind so fuzzy the drug would no longer help.

Conte raised his head and hollered, "Rook!"

Neither voice nor gunfire answered.

Conte unhooked the Ingram from the leather lanyard. He held it by the barrel, cocked his arm, and threw hard as he could, grunting with the pain the exertion drew from his leg. The machine pistol caromed off a bamboo stalk and clunked to the ground fifteen yards away.

"There's my goddamned gun." Conte's voice sounded strange even to him. "I'm hurt bad, you son of a bitch.

Come in and get me." He moved out silently, weaving ten yards laterally from where he guessed Rook to be.

"You bastard, what do you want?" Conte screamed. He had no difficulty sounding anguished. He was moving steadily among the stalks now.

"You got another gun," Rook's gutteral voice suddenly accused.

Conte stopped for a moment and peered in the direction of the noise. "So do you, you bastard." He could see nothing but the sameness of the densely packed green stalks. He moved a few steps. "I'm telling you, I'm cut up. I need help."

"Come out where I can see you." The voice had not moved. "Hands up."

Conte dug out the .45. He cradled it against his leg to muffle the clack of the charging slide, then brought the gun up in both hands. He could still see no sign of Rook.

Then he realized he was staring directly at the man.

Only a sliver of his knobby dark skull was visible; the rest of him was eclipsed by the bamboo shoots, and a good thirty yards separated them.

"I don't know where the hell I am," Conte shouted, moving on. "I'll come out if you tell me where to come out to." He was circling now, but he saw Rook turn to follow his voice.

"Hands up right now," the big *mestizo* ordered. "I can see where you are."

He was bluffing; he had to be. Conte was halfway around him and moving in. Ahead were three stalks that were close enough together to share roots. Conte made their cover, holding his breath for silence.

He peered around the bamboo, holding the .45 in both hands. Rook bellowed, "Where are you?"

"Right here," Conte said.

Rook spun around and brought up the Russian assault rifle, but Conte was already planted in a spread-legged firing-range stance, the .45 precocked for accuracy and fully extended in both hands, elbows locked—and Conte had the man's big, ugly, dark head floating perfectly above the open sights. Conte shot him in the forehead from maybe fifteen feet, and the heavy slug cored a third eye atop where his bushy eyebrows met.

Rook seemed to freeze in place. He held the assault rifle at port arms, and his wide eyes were locked on Conte, his mouth open as if he had been about to speak but forgot what he was going to say. Conte remembered shooting the man in Yugoslavia and the way the impact of the bullet hardly slowed him. Something thick and red and gray was leaking from the hole in Rook's forehead.

He lowered the AKM and let it fall from his fingers, then turned his back to Conte and walked into a bamboo stalk. His head bounced back from it and he sat down hard, legs splayed on either side of the green trunk, and then his chin fell forward and the gore from the hole in his head began to drip in soft plops on his bare chest.

Conte let his breath out in a long sigh. He had to see to business right then, before the aftershock set in.

The sheathed machete was similar to the ones the Pygmies carried. Conte drew it and slit the waistband of Rook's cammie slacks and stripped them off the corpse. He'd need the material for a wrapper.

He had an idea for a gift—for Vancouver.

Rook's body was lying on its side now. Conte pinned Rook's head with his foot to steady the target, then drew the machete back over his head in both hands.

Chapter Sixteen

"Undress," Vancouver said in his flat steely voice.

Melinda Bannister was sitting with her elbows on the mesh patio table, her chin cupped in her palms. She looked up at him and said, "No."

The sun was directly overhead now, and the sliver of ocean visible from the patio sparkled like an amethyst. Vancouver stared at it. "If you don't, I'll rape you."

"Would you like that?" Melinda said coldly. "Would you get more pleasure if you had to force me?"

Vancouver stared at her. "About the same." He swept his eyes over her: she wore khaki Bermuda shorts and an elasticized tube top that molded to her breasts.

"You like to hurt people."

"No," Vancouver said, with what sounded like patience. "I like to know where I stand. Now undress."

"You really will rape me if I don't, won't you." It was not a question. "You don't mind hurting me."

"That's right," Vancouver said.

Melinda stared past him. Eula, the Negrito maid, was standing outside the door of the house near the edge of the patio, talking to a Negrito man; Melinda thought she recognized him as another of the servants, but was not sure.

Vancouver followed her gaze. "It doesn't matter if they see." He looked at her. "Does it?"

"You bastard."

"Get undressed."

For a long moment she returned his look. Then she

stood abruptly and crossed her arms to the waistband of the
tube top, yanking it angrily up over her full breasts. She
skinned down the shorts and the bikini panties she wore
underneath, then stood facing him, arms akimbo. From near
the house Eula stared at her balefully.

"Over there." Vancouver pointed to the grassy verge
beside the patio. She went to it wordlessly, lying down on
her back and spreading her legs, her face set in a tight mask.
Vancouver nodded, as if the pose were just right, and began
to undo the buttons of his shirt.

She tried to lie rigid when he touched her, and managed
it for a minute or a little more, but as his hands and tongue
moved over her body, her hips began to move like they were
detached from her control, thrusting up to meet his caresses.
By the time she felt his length slide up inside her, she could
not stop herself any longer and did not want to try. She felt
the grass scratching at her back and ass, and his bulk
pressing her down, and then the spasms of pleasure
pounding at her insides like hurricane surf on hard-pack
beach sand.

Her eyes were screwed shut, and it took some seconds
for the transcending convulsions to abate so she was aware
of the word she was moaning again and again: "Bastard,
bastard, bastard . . ."

When she opened her eyes, she was looking up at
Eula. The Negrito was standing beside them. Her expression might more properly have belonged on a dowager who
just found dogshit on her shoe, and it would have been
comical in other circumstances.

"This come," she said in a dead voice, and dropped
something on the lawn beside them.

"Go away," Vancouver said. Eula moved out of
Melinda's line of sight. "No, stay here." Eula stopped and
stood docile as a dairy cow.

Melinda felt Vancouver slide out of her. She sat up. He still had an erection, she noticed. He was crouched naked over what looked like a pile of dirty rags.

Then Melinda realized the cloth was stiff with blood. "What is it?" Her voice was tremulous.

"Let's find out." He pulled the flaps of the bundle apart and threw them to either side.

Rook's head lay over on one ear, facing Melinda. The skin looked dried and shriveled, so the face was skull-like, the vacant eyes staring sightlessly out of deep-sunk sockets. Around the hole in the forehead was a rim of dried blood.

The head had been chopped off neatly at the Adam's apple, and the end of the spine, the windpipe, and various veins and arteries hung out of what had been the neck, like the wires of a transistor radio that had been run over by a truck. Everything was washed with red, as if Rook's head had contained nothing but blood, damned up like a beaver creek. Some of it still glistened wetly.

Melinda Bannister screamed. Vancouver turned almost absently and slapped her face, not very hard. She stopped screaming and vomited all over her chest.

Vancouver paid no attention. He was studying the head as if it were a sacred relic.

He still had the erection when he stood. Eula frowned at it as if it were an unruly child. "Where did this come from?"

"Found it. Over front of the house." She gestured vaguely.

"Did you see anyone? A white man."

The Negrito shook her head. "Not no one."

Melinda looked at the mess all over her and retched again.

Vancouver glanced at her. "Get Naruta," he ordered the Negrito.

"Naruta gone."

"Go to the village and tell the men to come."

Eula didn't move.

"Did you hear what I said?"

"Won't come," Eula said sullenly. Melinda had gotten herself under control and was trying to wipe herself off.

"Why not?" Vancouver demanded.

"No more. Too much. Too much blood, too much dead."

"All right," Vancouver said calmly. "Get to the village."

"That's right. I get." She looked past the stoic blond man. "Good-bye, Lady."

Melinda was still hyperventilating. Vancouver stood with his hands on his hips, staring down at Rook's severed head and looking mildly nonplussed. Melinda pressed both palms to the grass and managed to get to her feet. She felt wetness on the inside of her thighs, and another wave of nausea passed over her.

"For the love of God," she said weakly. "Get rid of that, please."

"All right." Vancouver bent and picked up the head in one hand, his palm cupped over the skull. He reared back and the head went spinning end over end into the trees.

Vancouver looked at his palm. There was a smear of red wetness in the middle of it. He turned and wiped it across Melinda's breasts. He was almost smiling.

"You sick son of a bitch," Melinda moaned. Her legs wouldn't work again, and she sat down in the grass. She felt filthy inside and out.

Vancouver left her there and turned toward the house.

Matt Conte sighted down the length of the Ingram, but it took concentrating and ten seconds for him to focus his eyes, and by that time his arms were trembling so badly he could not hold the machine pistol steady, even when he rested his forearms on a limb. Sweat dripped from his forehead to mix with tears of frustration; he pulled up the hem of his shirt and wiped angrily at his face.

Vancouver—it had to be him—stood nude, his back to Conte, no more than fifty yards distant.

Conte tried to bring the Ingram up again, but his arm muscles would not cooperate. It was a long shot for a handgun, but Conte could regularly score fist-sized clusters at the distance with the .45, and the Ingram was significantly more accurate. But now it was outside the realm of risk. His body was rebelling at his control; he could no longer trust his vision or his strength beyond the most elemental applications. In his condition, firing at this distance was a pure crapshoot.

And if he missed, he was a dead man.

He lay prone on the long forked branch of an apple tree near the edge of the clearing, twenty feet above the ground. The effort of climbing to the perch had started the gash in his leg bleeding again, and he could feel the warm thick blood worming down his skin. If he was not close enough to shoot, it was time to move on. Yet it was such a relief to lie down, even for a few moments. . . .

Conte dug the vial out of the pocket of the windbreaker. There were only two Dexedrine tablets left, and he felt a chill wash of panic. He popped them in his mouth, but he had no saliva left, and he had to chew them to bitter powder before he could get them down.

He had been there for about ten minutes—long enough to confirm the presence and position of Vancouver and the Bannister woman. He had watched her strip naked and open her legs to the well-built blond man, had seen her quickly ignited passion flicker and take flame and build to conflagration, and he had been disgusted. Sighting down the quivering barrel of the Ingram he considered for a moment the simple solution, a trigger-pull away: of the thirty rounds in the pistol's clip, enough would find the target, and both threats—Vancouver's deadly arts and Melinda Bannister's deadly information—would be eradicated, and Conte would be left in peace.

But that was the fever working on his mind, and in any case by the time he considered the idea the little black woman had delivered the grisly package Conte had flung into the middle of the clearing fronting the open house, and Vancouver had moved out of Conte's clear sightline to unwrap it. Conte hoped to hell the contents worked on Vancouver as he meant them to.

The penicillin had only slowed the progress of the infection: the ragged edge of the wound was discoloring and had begun to ooze pus. Conte's forehead was hot to his own touch, but the chills rippled through his body constantly now; the effort of controlling them cost a lot of strength.

Realistically, he gave himself an hour. By then the infection and shock, or Vancouver, would take him out. He checked the Rolex.

It was eleven in the morning.

So he had to bring Vancouver out into the open, had to put the other man on the offensive. If Vancouver chose to stay in the house, to keep his back to the wall, he could wait Conte out.

Whatever tiny chance of survival Conte had depended on the possibility of drawing Vancouver to neutral ground—or into ambush.

Melinda Bannister was still huddled naked on the grass at the edge of the patio. She sat with her legs drawn up, her arms around her knees and her chin resting on them, and she was rocking back and forth and making the same kind of monotonic noise a mother uses to calm a child with a skinned knee. She would be useless until this was over, Conte thought bitterly. The hell with it; the thought of her help disgusted him anyway.

Vancouver came out on the patio again. He wore khaki twill slacks, a loose white T-shirt, and blue Nike tennis shoes; as far as Conte could see, he was unarmed. He glanced incuriously at Melinda Bannister, then turned away from her and stood motionless for nearly a minute, like an animal sniffing out a new environment. Conte tried to bring up the Ingram again, and could not find the strength. At that moment Vancouver turned and seemed to look directly at him, and Conte felt a quick bloodrush of panic.

Vancouver turned and walked in the other direction, passing Melinda Bannister without glancing at her. When Conte came out of the tree, his bad leg folded up on him and he went down, breathing hard with the pain and effort. Holding his head upright seemed the utmost exertion, closing his eyes and lying down just for a few moments the most sublime bliss.

Instead he used the trunk of the apple tree and the crutch to lever himself erect, and hobbled back into the rain forest.

When she stood up again, she had to take a step to keep her balance, and the high sun seemed too bright, painfully glary. Her gait was stiff when she crossed the patio, placing her bare feet on the warm stones as if they were eggshells. At the threshold, she called, "Eula!" Her voice sounded like someone else's, but it did not matter because no one answered her. When she turned on the water in the shower, she was acutely aware of the hum of the pump motor.

She scrubbed herself meticulously and with total absorption; it seemed very important that she go over every

square inch of her body with soap and the cleansing sluice
of hot water. It took a long time, and she might have stayed
under the spray longer if the water had not begun to turn
cool. She stared curiously at her own image in the mirror,
and suddenly she was trembling so badly she had to sit
down on the toilet seat.

She shook her head violently in denial, but she knew
the truth: the touch of a man would never be the same again.
It would remind her—of Vancouver's cold, demeaning flesh
penetrating without touching, of the severed head lying on
its ear in the grass. It would always be there for her.

Unless she did something. Unless she made it right
again.

Melinda Bannister rubbed at her eyes and opened them
wide. She had gone into shock; the scientist in her
understood that. She sat still for a long time, her head
between her knees. When she stood she was still wobbly,
but she felt rational, almost calm.

She pushed damp hair out of her face but did not bother
to brush it. There was more important business to see to.

Conte spent five precious minutes on the recon and
another three rigging the clothesline booby trap. The
hardest part was climbing the tree. That ate up another
couple of minutes.

By then he could hear Vancouver coming down the
trail.

Conte had forgotten about the fishline he had taken
from Ferdinand's pack, and he would not have remembered
if it hadn't fallen out of the pocket of his windbreaker as he
bent to clear a low limb. It was a spool of maybe fifty yards
of four-pound-test monofilament. Conte hefted it on his
palm and got an idea.

The pair of wild apple trees flanked the trail, about two

feet apart; the lowest branches were a yard above the ground, so you had to duck to pass under them. There was thick rain-forest underbrush to either side of the path, so although you could beat your way around the trees, it would cost time and noise.

Conte went on through.

He crouched on the other side and took a half-dozen turns around one of the trunks, then knee-walked across the path to the other tree, unspooling the thin line. He pulled it taut, tied it off, then pulled back.

From two feet away, the colorless line was nearly invisible. If a man was bent in an awkward position, and worrying about ambush on the other side of the trees, there was even more chance he'd miss the trap.

Conte had to use arms only to get up into the tree; when he tried to get leverage with his bad leg, its only response was a spasm of pain. He pulled himself up branch over branch, until he reached a limb that extended out above the trail. He got the Ingram loose from the windbreaker, extending it in front of him as he shinnied out on the branch.

If the clothesline just slowed Vancouver for a moment, it would give Conte time to line a close shot on him. But that might not be enough. Conte knew his arms were so shaky that he'd need a hell of a short range to score.

Point-blank would be ideal.

So he had to be ready. If he got really lucky and the line cut Vancouver, or tripped him up, Conte would have to come out of the tree. He did not want to think about what that might do to his leg. He thought only of the sequence of movements, went over them again and again in his mind: drop on the bastard, jab him with the muzzle of the Ingram automatic, and inject a full magazine into his guts.

He had just settled on the limb when he heard Vancouver coming.

The guy wasn't going out of his way to keep down the sound of his approach. Conte heard a branch snap, legs shushing through underbrush—and then Vancouver came around a turn in the path, ten steps uptrail from Conte.

Conte thought about lining the Ingram on him and did not. Rushing the play could send it all to hell. He held completely still, did not even breathe.

Vancouver moved down the trail, paused for a split second directly below Conte. He seemed to sniff the air, but then he ducked to go under the apple-tree branches blocking the way.

Conte started to roll off the limb—and saw Vancouver hold. Conte hugged the rough bark, most of his weight already over the side.

Vancouver withdrew his head from under the branches, stood erect, and looked up at Conte—

And Conte let go of the limb.

He held the Ingram out in front of him like a lance as he dove for Vancouver, and he saw the man twist away and raise a hand. Conte tried to correct in midair, flopping like a fish. He was plummeting sickeningly and the twenty-foot drop was endless.

The ground was hard as slate. A lightning bolt of pain pierced Conte's leg and he screamed; a blinding white light blotted out his vision. Something cracked into his head, very hard. The noise stopped, and the light went out.

Melinda Bannister pushed through a thicket of underbrush. Foliage scratched at her legs and broken branches dug into the soles of her bare feet, but she did not notice. It was almost midday, and the leafy roof overhead spread a languorously dim greenish light over most of the forest floor, though a few yards ahead shafts of sunlight cut down into a clearing.

Melinda did not notice the open space until she pushed into it, and saw the Negritos.

There were seven of them, all women, spread out in a line with Eula at their center. She had gotten rid of her serving-girl tapa skirt, and like the others was wearing only a whitish loincloth that covered her sex and little else.

Melinda looked at the women and drew herself up short, pushing a clot of hair out of her face. Her forehead was damp to the touch, and felt feverish against the back of her hand. Eula stared at her with the same baleful, accusatory look she had worn at the house.

The expression was echoed on every other face.

"Eula, please," Melinda said. She could not catch her breath. "Did he come this way?"

Eula stared at her.

"The other man," Melinda panted. "Is he dead?"

The other women might have been wax figures.

"Please," Melinda pleaded. "Help me, Eula."

Not very far away, a man howled with pain.

The cry seemed to go on for a long time, and until its echo died none of the Negrito women moved. Melinda felt as if her own joints were frozen in place. She gulped air and started to say, "You must help me, please. He'll kill . . ."

Eula turned away and slipped back into the forest, and the other women followed like novitiates bound to a vow of silence.

Melinda stared after them. She closed her eyes, breathed deeply and slowly, opened her eyes again and blinked.

On the ground, where the women had been standing, something shined silver among the ferns.

Melinda crossed the clearing and looked down and remembered where she was going, what she had to do.

She had to make him pay, or everywhere she went they

would look at her as the Negrito women had, and they would know. More than that, *she* would know. She would see him reflected in the faces of everyone, everywhere she looked, and they would see his mark on her.

She could not solve everything; it was too late for that. Even after he paid she would still see his image, sprung from her mind's eye no matter how she denied it. But when he paid, she would be able to live with the vision.

Conte opened his eyes and knew he was alive, because he hurt too badly to be dead.

He had been out ten minutes, and he knew that timing had been no accident. Vancouver's blow to his head had been as delicate as a surgeon's first scalpel cut, designed to hurt him and put him under, but not to take him out of action.

It had accomplished the first part very well. Conte's head pulsed, and there was a soft, pulpy damp spot near the base of his skull. His leg wound felt like someone had stuck a knife in it and was twisting the blade.

The business with the clothesline trap had been a stupid waste of time, and Conte should have known that before he tried it. The son of a bitch owned this damned island, and of course he knew all the hiding places.

Open space, Conte remembered. He needed open space for the facedown. Maybe it would balance the odds a little. The cogon-grass meadow, the mangrove swamp at Socorro's southern tip, or the beach . . .

Or did Vancouver figure that would be his play?

The bastard was doing games, sure. There was no other explanation for Conte's continued existence. He was being played like a fish, and fighting the lure only set the hook deeper.

So the hell with second-guessing the guy. The beach

was the perimeter, the way out. The beach was an end—or a beginning.

Conte pulled himself painfully to his feet. Vancouver had left him both his guns, the arrogant bastard. Conte would feed the guy the Ingram's magazine, one slug at a time. He swayed, then lurched into the forest.

He found Vancouver on the downslope side of the bamboo thicket, standing over the bodies of the Negrito couple, arms folded, no more than twenty yards away. Vancouver looked up and nodded, as if satisfied that Conte was ambulatory again.

Conte stared stupidly at the expressionless blond man for what seemed like a very long time. Vancouver stood loosely, hands away from his sides, like some fast-draw artist in a bad Western. Conte set his feet apart and moved his hands away from the Ingram, waiting for the other man to make the first move. . . .

Then the preservation instinct broke through the delirium's fog, and Conte remembered to notice that the other man was still unarmed and the hell with fair fights, and he grabbed with fingers that felt thick as link sausages at the Ingram hanging from his neck. He reached the trigger, squeezed hard, and felt the machine pistol buck and torque in his stiff hands.

When the clip was empty and the gun fell silent, Vancouver had dematerialized. Conte stared at where he had been, ears straining to pick up the sound of his retreat, and neither saw nor heard anything.

Move on; he had to move on. He remembered: open space. *Why was he still alive anyway?* he thought, angry for no rational reason. Why not kill him and have it over with? His legs were wobbling like they had been deboned. He was carrying too much weight. *Too many guns,* he thought foolishly. *Only need one gun—only one bullet, if it hits right*. The Ingram was several times more gun than the Colt, but the .45 was his gun. That was important in a fight—you had to have your own gun.

Conte unclipped the Ingram and threw it into the bamboo grove, then unholstered the .45, checked the clip, and worked the charging lever, knowing he was being stubborn and perhaps stupid and the hell with it. . . .

Two hundred yards further down the slope, right after he became aware of the sound of the surf somewhere ahead, Conte saw the flash of Vancouver's white T-shirt, a couple of dozen feet off to his right. This time he did not miss a beat in raising the Colt in both hands and squeezing off a shot. But the T-shirt would not hold still above the open sight, and before he could aim again his arms gave out. The gun slipped out of his fingers into the thick bed of ferns at his feet, and Conte, instantly panicked, dropped to hands and knees and pawed frantically at the fronds until his dead hands closed over the automatic's butt.

By then, of course, Vancouver was gone.

Conte may have seen him once or twice more as he bushwhacked down the slope; something imposed itself on his vision, and it may have been real or hallucination. He had to get to the beach; that was what counted. That was important.

On the beach dwelt salvation.

It would end on the beach.

The infection was overtaking him like a runaway boxcar on a 6 percent grade. His filthy, blood-encrusted clothing was sopping with sweat, though his skin felt cold and dead to the touch, and the shivering was beyond any control. Blood streaked with green pus squeezed from between the lips of the long knife gash in his thigh, and the skin around it was starting to blacken. In his head, rational thought fought a futile battle with fever-driven delirium.

The dial of the Rolex swam before Conte's eyes. He lifted his left wrist with his right hand and held the watch a few inches from his nose.

It was a couple of minutes before noon.

One of them would be dead before the hour was out.

You did not give up: the thought seared through his addled mind. If you gave up you were dead, and after that there was nothing. You fought to stay alive. You survived.

The trees parted in front of him and he stepped through their curtain onto the sand. It was surreally white, a color so brilliant it did not exist in nature. The sand was soft and sucked at his feet, and it was shifting and swirling and in constant motion, like the water beyond.

The water: he had to make the water. You did not drink seawater—he remembered that with a savvy grin—but he would lie in it for a little while and feel better. He could make the water. Ten steps: five with the left, five with the right.

The crutch would not work in the sand, so he had to crawl. It made a furrow as he dragged it behind him. He got as far as the wet hard pack; sand gritted into the open wound. Conte shook his head and stared down at it.

He was going to die.

The rain forest parted once more, and Vancouver stepped out on the sand. Conte raised his head and saw the slim featureless blond man standing ten feet away and above him, arms folded as before.

Conte looked at his hands and the gun was not there; terror jolted through his guts. He remembered: he had to holster it to drag himself across the sand. He fumbled it out, but it slid from his fingers, and when he tried to pick it up, the task simply went beyond his abilities. All of this seemed to take a very long time.

He tipped up his head once more and focused on

Vancouver's motionless figure, and then, with breathtaking spontaneity the delirium fog in his mind thinned and dissipated, like wine turned to water by a conjurer's art, and Conte saw everything with unreal clarity.

He wondered: was this the compensation—this eleventh-hour purity of mind and eye and purpose—was this the benefice for death?

Vancouver moved out to the center of the strip of albescent beach and said, "Come out, Melinda. This is finished now."

Vancouver did not look back, but through his legs Conte saw Melinda Bannister come out of the rain forest.

She wore what must have been Vancouver's shirt—this instantly angered Conte—because it was several sizes too large for her, voluminous. The tails hung to just above her bare knees. Her hair was a tangled limp nest, and the face it framed smouldered with fury or hate or vengeance. Conte watched the cloth stretch as her breasts raised with a deep breath; it made a chilling rattling sound.

All of this Conte saw with manic vivid clarity.

"Stay where you are," Vancouver said to the woman, still staring down at Conte.

Melinda walked toward them.

"I said stay put." There was mild annoyance in his tone.

Melinda was a few steps from them now.

Vancouver frowned slightly and turned away from Conte, and Conte saw Melinda Bannister's hand come out from within the draped folds of the too-large shirt. She held a machete, underhand and blade up. Conte saw her double her grip and lunge, and Vancouver twisted away but not quickly enough, so his side was presented to her. She put all her weight into the thrust, driving the blade into him to the right of his navel, below the rib cage. Conte saw the thin tip of the machete cut through cotton and skin and muscle, and it seemed like the man sucked the blade into him, like a boor might inhale a strand of spaghetti.

Vancouver's blue eyes went wide, but no expression—fear nor shock nor pain—marred his granite features, and he did not go down. Blood oozed out around the knife blade, and when Melinda let go of the haft, the metal stayed where it was.

Vancouver looked down at the blood and up at Melinda, and grabbed her throat in both hands.

Melinda opened her mouth to scream and she could not. Her knee jerked up and bounced harmlessly off Vancouver's thigh. Her tongue was sticking out. It looked too red, as if she had been eating cinnamon candy.

The .45 lay at Conte's knees, and he picked it up, natural as life. A little sand adhered to the barrel, which he brushed off. The bore looked clear, but Conte was concerned that if even a few grains got inside it would score badly the first time fired. He smiled foolishly: that didn't matter now.

Blood was soaking obscenely into the front of Vancouver's slacks. He took his right hand off the woman's neck, steadied her with his left, and drove his fist into her face. Her nose exploded in a splash of redness. Vancouver hit her again in the same place, then flung her away. She fell limp and did not move, except for the stream of red blood flowing into white sand. Everything was too bright.

Vancouver put both hands around the curved blade of the machete and drew it out of his side. Blood dribbled from the wound.

Conte flopped down on his stomach in the wet sand, propped up his elbows, and held the .45 in both hands, thumbing back the hammer. At the sound Vancouver turned and raised the machete over his head and charged.

Conte rolled away and fired blind, then rolled again. Something slammed into Conte's wrist, and the .45 knocked free and arced through the clear air and plunked into the water at Conte's back.

Conte grappled for Vancouver's ankle, and the other man scuttled away. Conte was startled. He took a deep ragged breath and looked over at him.

The blond man was sitting up, a couple of yards away. His left leg was straight out in front of him, and there was blood on his khaki pants, where Conte's wild shot had found his kneecap. More blood soaked his side and puddled in his lap. The machete that the Bannister woman had put into him lay out of his reach. The woman herself was another ten yards up the beach, lying in the bloody sand. Maybe she was dead—and the hell with her.

Conte stabbed the crutch deep into the sand and used its support to climb to his feet. Vancouver watched him through dead blue eyes as he circled around. Conte bent warily for the machete.

He got hold of the haft, and Vancouver's hand shot out and closed around the crutch and yanked it out from under him.

Conte hacked at Vancouver's arm and missed, and the handle of the machete, slick with blood, flew out of his fingers and away from them. He went down hard, slamming his good knee into Vancouver's midsection, and Vancouver grunted. Conte rolled away, made it to hands and knees.

Vancouver spit blood into the sand and crawled after him, dragging his shattered leg in the hard pack.

Conte scuttled away on the heels of his hands. Vancouver stopped, shook his blond head like a punchy boxer, then came on again.

Conte drew up the thick branch that he was using for a crutch, and said, "Keep coming, you son of a bitch."

Vancouver got his good leg under him, and he looked at Conte with something that may have been a smile—and then he pushed off, launched himself at Conte.

Conte swung the crutch into Vancouver's ribs and then the other man was on top of him, one hand clawing at Conte's face, the thumb groping for an eye socket, the other hand crushing his throat and voice box.

Conte brought the crutch around, held the branch with fists about a foot apart, and broke it down on Vancouver's head. Vancouver expelled hot fetid breath into his face. His thumb gouged into Conte's Adam's apple, and Conte could not pull air into his lungs.

Conte hit him again, and a third time. Wood cracked into bone, but there was no power to the blows. His lungs were on fire, and his eyes would not focus. He hit Vancouver again, and the stick fractured but did not break.

Vancouver's forehead cracked into Conte's chin, and the pressure on his throat eased. He pushed, rolled away from the blond man's bulk. Vancouver caught his breath, expelled it in a howl of rage and hurt, and clawed back toward him.

Conte wielded the splintered branch, holding it by the end with both hands like a baseball bat, and brought it around with every ounce of strength remaining to him. The branch caught the side of Vancouver's head and one end broke off and flew across the beach, end over end. Blood came from near Vancouver's ear. Conte lunged at him, hit him again with the one-foot length of wood that was left, hit him a third time.

Vancouver rolled over on his back and gasped. Conte slammed the club into the middle of Vancouver's face. There was a choking rattling sound, and blood bubbled from Vancouver's broken mouth. His entire body convulsed as if it had been jolted by a massive current.

Conte raised the club over his head—and let it fall out of his hands. Vancouver was not breathing anymore. Conte looked around for something else to do.

Melinda Bannister lay motionless ten yards away, the man's shirt rucked up around her waist. He would see to her now; that would be sensible. He crawled in her direction.

But he never came close to making it, and the last thing Conte saw was Melinda Bannister's perfect long legs, splayed awkwardly, and brown as snuff against the nacre sand.

Manila

The 12th of August

Miss Paradise had gone native. "It's called a *terno,* she said. "I got it in the *mestiza* market." The dress was fashioned of brightly printed cotton, with a full pleated skirt, a deeply scooped neckline, and butterfly sleeves. Her pellucid platinum hair was done in a simple fall, and her tan had deepened in the last week. She looked wonderful.

Matt Conte felt like rewarmed shit.

He had argued with two doctors and half a dozen nurses before he finally gave in and agreed to stay in the hospital one more day. The fever had still not broken completely, and there was a dull ache where the cut was and purplish bruises all up and down the leg, but they told him he'd recover completely, and beyond that he didn't give a shit. He was sufficiently depressed without the hospital confinement, and he needed badly to escape the odor of death.

"How are you, Matt?" Dennison said, with evident concern. He looked impossibly cool, despite the fact that the central air-conditioning in the Philippine General Hos-

pital in Ermita had chosen that morning to shut itself down.
The white polo shirt he wore looked crisp as iceberg lettuce.

Miss Paradise brushed a teasing hand across his
forehead, so her fingertips just touched his skin. "He's
okay," she said. "I think he's dogging it. What say we dock
his pay?"

Conte sighed. "Nice to see you too, honey." But then
he added seriously: "Thanks for coming. It is good to see
you."

"We've been here since yesterday, Hot Shot," Miss
Paradise said. "They said you were too crazy to talk."

"Maybe I was," Conte said slowly. He remembered
Vancouver's fist closed over his windpipe, the terror of
being unable to breathe. He could not completely shake the
image of Ferdinand, faceless and gutted like a stag . . .

"Cilla." His voice was tight. "Did she make it?"

"She's out of danger," Dennison said. "The doctors
are confident she'll recover completely. She's been under
sedation, in and out of consciousness, pretty much since
you took her to the hospital, but her surgeon told me this
morning that he'll be cutting off the medication today. He
thinks she'll be awake and able to receive visitors tomorrow."

"Then she doesn't know about her father," Conte said,
half to himself. "I'll take care of it." It was a small partial
payment of the huge debt he owed to her—and to
Ferdinand's memory.

"I understand, Matt," Dennison said. "In the meantime, I'll make certain she isn't disturbed."

Conte worked the bridge of his nose between thumb
and forefinger. "Fill me in on the rest of it." He shook a
cigarette from the pack on the night table.

Miss Paradise lit it with a disposable Bic. "After you
killed Vancouver, you decided to take a nap on the beach.

You didn't know it at the time, but the Negritos had abandoned Vancouver, so once he was dead you were safe."

"What about the Bannister woman? The last thing I remember—"

"She wasn't hurt too badly," Dennison said. "Vancouver broke her nose, knocked out a front tooth, and left a few bruises, but she came around after a while. She made sure you were still breathing—and that Vancouver wasn't— then went back to the house and used Vancouver's radio transceiver. It took a while before she found the frequency, but she eventually got a response to her Mayday from the Air Force's Edwin Andrew Base at Zamboanga on Mindaneo. They had a doctor in an ambulance chopper and to you within an hour. Those Air Force boys know how to respond to emergencies."

"They're cute, too," Miss Paradise said. "Anyway," she went on, "we lucked out twice. First, she was never pumped for the top secret defense information she was privy to, because Vancouver planned to sell her and had no personal interest in it. Second, she had the wits to give the Air Force a good story: she was kidnapped, but she couldn't tell any more without violating security. When Military Intelligence checked with the FBI, they were informed she was telling the truth, which in a way she was. And when they get around to investigating on Socorro at length, all they'll find is a pile of rotting corpses and some pissed-off Pygmies."

"Well I'll be Goddamned," Conte said disgustedly. "Are you telling me that she gets out of this caper without a scratch?"

"Not exactly. She's been stripped of her security clearance. She can't work for her husband, and no one else will hire her now. Within a few years what she knows will be public information anyway, and after that she'll never be a threat again."

"I thought the whole business had been hushed up. I know we don't need the publicity."

"There was none." Dennison smiled faintly. "It was my unilateral decision that Melinda Bannister was a security risk." The smile broadened. "I also thought she deserved to suffer some kind of punishment. So I made a phone call."

"You've got a lot of friends, Dennison."

"Count on that," Miss Paradise said.

"What about the husband?" Conte stretched to reach the ashtray on the night table and felt a stab of pain in his leg.

Dennison's smile dimmed. "He wanted her fetched back to him, and she's been fetched back to him."

"He got what he paid for," Miss Paradise said.

"But not what he wanted," Dennison added softly.

That was the part that bothered Conte. He had no sympathy for Lawrence Bannister; guys like him put themselves on the spot. But Melinda Bannister, who in the end loved no one but herself, that still ate at him. . . .

"There's something else, Matt," Dennison cut into his thoughts. "I've got some bad news."

Conte knew what was coming. Before leaving for Rome a week earlier, he had told Dennison what Weepy Moyers had told him in the coffee shop of El San Juan. Dennison had promised to check it out with his contacts, as a personal favor to Conte.

"Moyers gave you straight info," Dennison said. "The Old Men have let it be known—subtly, not through the usual channels—that they would not mind if you died. There isn't paper out on you."

"Not yet," Miss Paradise added sweetly. Conte scowled at her.

"But everyone knows there's money in it," Dennison went on smoothly. "Now that Bressio is out of the way, it looks like the Old Men are seeing to loose ends." Dennison cleared his throat. "There is also a chance the Old Men have some idea of what you are doing now, and who you're working for—and they may not approve."

"You're going to have to watch your butt, boy," Miss Paradise said.

"You will have to be careful, Matt," Dennison said seriously. "You'll want to stay out of circulation until you're a hundred percent again. There's a place for you at the compound."

"I won't involve you in my troubles—not when the shooting starts."

"I wouldn't worry about it, Hot Shot."

She had a point. He remembered the way she had handled herself in the last battle, in a Nevada desert canyon.

"Thanks," he said. "To you both."

Miss Paradise surprised him by bending and lightly brushing his lips with hers, and for some minutes after they left he still felt her fine hair tracing across his forehead. But after a time the depression closed in on him again. It was not the news that men with guns were likely to start showing up on his back track again; he'd expected that. Nor was it the leg; he'd been assured that there would be complete healing and no loss of function, and his sense of his own body confirmed that.

But Melinda Bannister stayed with him, like a warlock's curse. He saw her grinding her pelvis up into Vancouver, and the mess she was a few minutes later, and he saw her when she put six inches of tempered steel through his guts. Conte lit another cigarette from the butt of the first, then ground it out in a saucer he had swiped from his breakfast tray.

He recalled a story from a long-ago high-school class; it had fascinated and repulsed him at the time. After sexual congress, the biology teacher said, the female black widow spider kills and eats her mate. He knew he would remember Melinda Bannister time and again for the rest of his life, and never without thinking of the spider story.

DENNISON'S WAR #3:
HELL ON WHEELS
by Adam Lassiter

The jackals are constantly on the prowl, and it isn't enough to lock and barricade the door. Occasionally you have to exterminate a few of the beasts. That's the role Dennison and his network of professional fighters dare to undertake—in a world going mad they get even.

Dennison's Warrior Chris Amado, trained by years of jungle rebel fighting, gets the call to combat the growing, vicious threat of outlaw motorcycle gangs. These wild-riding cadres of murder, crime and destruction are manipulated by steel-edged businessmen who have honed their operations into multimillion dollar crime rings that defy all state and local law enforcement agencies.

Now these territorial outlaw crime lords are threatening to unite in one slithering chain of power and violence which will squeeze a deadly griplock on the whole country. Unless Chris Amado can lead Dennison's Warriors on a wild ride of their own—to swift, hard justice.

Don't miss the next DENNISON'S WAR adventure, HELL ON WHEELS, on sale May 15th wherever Bantam Books are sold.

SPECIAL
MONEY SAVING
OFFER

Now you can have an up-to-date listing of Bantam's hundreds of titles plus take advantage of our unique and exciting bonus book offer. A special offer which gives you the opportunity to purchase a Bantam book for only 50¢. Here's how!

By ordering any five books at the regular price per order, you can also choose any other single book listed (up to a $4.95 value) for just 50¢. Some restrictions do apply, but for further details why not send for Bantam's listing of titles today!

Just send us your name and address plus 50¢ to defray the postage and handling costs.

DON'T MISS
THESE CURRENT
Bantam Bestsellers